A SAINT *in* OLD LYME

A SAINT *in* OLD LYME

Elizabeth Brown

RESOURCE *Publications* · Eugene, Oregon

A SAINT IN OLD LYME

Resource Publications
An Imprint of Wipf and Stock Publishers
199 W. 8th Ave., Suite 3
Eugene, OR 97401

www.wipfandstock.com

PAPERBACK ISBN: 979-8-3852-2603-0
HARDCOVER ISBN: 979-8-3852-2604-7
EBOOK ISBN: 979-8-3852-2605-4

09/03/24

1

Jane, 1950

September 2

OH, JENNIE! MY SISTER, my soul, imbibe these words. I write for you, pray my words reach you. These times, oh, these weary times, a woman's travail. I'm of the flesh. My soul thirsts. I feast on small matters, the gable window and beveled glass, the prism of colors— a glow of amber, emerald, gold, a bellowing brightness, glittering and glamorous—a showcase of divinity beyond my grasp. I pray my words pierce your soul, Jennie, and you come to realize I'm with child. I'll be a mother, soon, and I'm lacking and thirsty for the spiritual, for our childhood, for the best of my days. I feel the life in me, stir and soothe. I feel the wilds of myself bursting to get out.

Later . . .

Good news! I found St. Faustina's diary on the bookshelf. The sun caught the gold trim on the binding. Faustina, like an old friend, an instrument of the holiest, Jennie. I return to Faustina, to my soul, to a purer state, to muster up courage, faith, to be anything but this. Is it true? Did the people come to me for healing? Is it a real memory? Did strangers pray to me? It's a faint memory, how they came and pitched tents on the beach, lit candles, and we prayed. When I returned from Mother of Mercy Home, John forbade it. He wants me healed for the baby. He turned the people away, put up a no trespassing sign. "It's too risky, Jane," he'd said. I should have protested. But I submitted. Now I'm altered, alien to myself, teetering on the edge of a precipice. John has me here, in the attic. It was the fall, the slip on the stairs. He tells me I'm taxed. Rest, Jane. Rest, he says. He worries for my health, for the health of our baby. He wants me settled, normal, unfettered by miracles and prayers. He doesn't understand my need for people, for the ocean, for you! If you were here, Jennie, you'd know what to say to your brother. Come home to me, Jennie!

September 3

No sun today. Only dark clouds and storms. Maribel brought me breakfast and went on about Anna, the coastal warnings, and then she left me alone with my anxious thoughts. John is flying out for a conference. The waves are mad. God's wrath. I tried reading Faustina, but the rough waters reminded me of the creek, the night of the séance and my transformation, before I became this. It was high tide, wild waters, white caps, those maddening gusts of wind making it impossible to light the candle. I wonder if you think of it, Jennie. I see us now, so clearly, young, unencumbered, feigned anger and hysteria, rushing to the edge of the water and retreating, hysterical, fists raised and aimed at your father's water gods, animated, possessed. We were invincible, impregnable. We were unmarred, innocent, protected by invisible guardians. The adults, lustful, inebriated and tarnished, circled the bonfire, indecipherable dark shapes in a blood orange glow, silhouettes in a blaze of flames, the crackle of wood, the leaping, lashing, tongues, the embers wafting, a cacophony of shrieks, the frenetic delirium, crazed spirits in the night. You were frantic, eager to see your father, convinced you saw him once in an upstairs window of the cottage. Little did I know, I, too, would lose a father in a few short years, one I never got to know.

John agreed to the seance, maybe to placate. He never liked the supernatural. I stood at the edge of the water, besieged, bewildered. An ethereal force took hold. I imagine myself walking past the fire, barely cognizant of the clinking bottles and glasses, trancelike, ears closed to the belligerent bellows, a call out to me, just before scaling the jetty. I have no actual memory of walking to the creek, or slipping over the edge. How is it possible? "No pulse," the paramedic said. I was declared dead. I returned like a resurrection. Is it true? I need to talk to you, Jennie. Once I knew it well, and now it's a distant memory, obtuse. I imagine the air in the attic is poisoning my mind, sucking out my soul.

Now I hear the creak on the attic stairs!

Update . . .

John returned earlier than usual. Storm Anna delayed his flight. He stayed with me for a bit. He sat on the edge of the bed, talked about the Hurricane of 1938. He was ten-years old. We were eight. Your father left us with a box of donuts, a fire burning, waved to us from the truck, heading off to the dock to secure his boat. We'd heard the foghorn. The hazy sun had barely broke through. The wind was picking up. He'd promised Eda he wouldn't' take her out. We evacuated and he was long gone by then. Then John's face when we got the news: *Taylor Wright is missing at sea.* John had just finished the last jelly donut. His mouth was open, powdered sugar coated his lips.

John stopped talking, settled his gaze on the beams above. He seemed pained, weary. He stood and moved over to the wicker chair. He was calm, reposed. Salt air and the mires of the marsh wafting off his clothes, his hair. Before he left, he kissed my stomach. A peck on the cheek. The door closed and my spirits dampened.

He loved me back then, Jennie, more than I knew.

He loves me now, even more, I suspect, and I should be content, here in our hideaway, Jennie. And John did touch it up so nicely for me, but for that one space in the corner by the bookshelf where the wallpaper remains. Maybe he figured it's so small an area, I'd never notice, or care. But I see it, and I wish I didn't. John blames everything on hormones. I'm silent. Like Mary, I keep all things in my heart.

Update . . .

The sun is back. John left, after all. The waves calmed. Anna went out to sea. I waited for him to return, and Maribel gave me the news. Like you, Jennie. Jesus, too, was abandoned in the garden and on the cross, left alone and thirsty for our salvation. Mine is simpler. I'm thirsty for a thing I can't define. I want to forgive, to be humbled. The way I was before my marriage and my pregnancy. Now I'm tarnished. I fall short. Father, oh, merciful God, help me to forgive. I forgive John. I love him, dearly, Jennie, I do. But he tells me I'm sick and taxed. "Rest, Jane. Rest," he insists. Now he's gone, again. Another conference. This one in Seattle. He promised he'd stay. I see the empty wicker chair. I see the lonely steam trunk filled with our dress-up clothes. I see the bookshelf we stenciled one summer with rabbits, birds, ferns, and flowers—and it saddens me, Jennie. Come home.

2

Jennie, 2020

Re: Canonization

Dear Bishop Monroe,

My name is Jennie Wright. I am the sister-in-law of Jane Wright, wife of Dr. John Wright. Perhaps you've read about her in the news. Although it's been some years since she passed into the Eternal Kingdom, fifty or so years ago, I still receive letters from her faithful followers. Some even pitch tents on the beach, light candles and pray to Jane Wright to intercede on their behalf, for whatever ails them. My brother prohibited it, put up a no trespassing sign, but then when I moved back, and he wasn't around, I took it down, and allowed them to come. Jane Wright has remained an anomaly, Your Reverence, and I just hope I can provide a full enough account of her experiences to convince you. I realize I am a lay person, albeit a devout Catholic in my final years. I've kept to the protocols and tried, without success, to appeal to our local clergy on this matter. The one time I did hear back was a brief recognition of the virtuosity of Jane Wright, but with little acknowledgement of her martyrdom or possible intercessory to God. The final letter, at the risk of spreading aspersions, could have very well been a form letter signed off by Father Samuel Macintosh.

You are Jane Wright's final hope, Your Reverence, as I've recently turned ninety and my days are numbered.

Let me begin by saying my purpose is a grand one, and, solely, of a divine nature. I'm appealing to you, and your committee (should it progress to that point), in the most true and profound manner with regards to Jane Wright who passed away, too soon, as martyred saints are apt to do. I, too, look upon my task as having an elevated purpose, a selfless devotion requiring a concerted amount of attention and focus. I pray I have enough energy to continue. I am in a weakened state, and my eyes are failing me. In my late years, I, too, have had visions, epiphanies, and realize now my life has been prolonged due to the intercession of my dearest friend, Jane Wright. I've prayed to her and spoken to her, and she's healed me. Indeed, I wouldn't be undertaking this lofty task if not for Jane. I was terminally ill and Jane came to me in a vision and assured me I would live. I woke fully recovered. When doctors completed tests and scans and could find no evidence of the disease they were stymied. Again, when I suffered a fatal stroke and was in a coma, Jane returned to me and assured me it was not my time. I woke fully recovered with no damage, cognitively, nor any signs of the stroke itself. The doctor notes are included with my correspondence.

Admittedly, in my younger years, I'd waffled in my belief. It was Jane, all Jane, who turned me wholly to God. Sadly, I lost touch of Jane. She lived a solitary life in prayer and deep faith. It was only later upon reviewing the past and with contemplation of Jane's miracles that I found my own faith. With all this in mind, Your Reverence, I pray that my words will prove to be worthy enough for your sanctity. I have a task in front of me, lofty, indeed. I am void of special talents or uniqueness, aside from knowing Jane Wright. Even my upbringing was one of privilege and I never suffered the ills of poverty like so many poor souls. Although my mother was widowed, she was a wise woman and raised us with solid Christian values and an unconditional love. Jane stayed with us during the summer. Our mothers were roommates in college and remained very close.

And now, I feel at this point it is beyond my capacity to cease writing and that Jane must have some part in my tenacity.

I begin with this: I am convinced my dearest friend, soul, kindred spirit, Jane Wright, I believe she should be canonized. I don't choose my words lightly, Your Reverence. No, it took me many years to admit. Now, I'm thoroughly convinced. I undergo this grand task, my final task, for Jane Wright and her daughter, Helen, and for so many others who might be healed by Jane's intercession.

I'll start simply: As is the manner of the saints, Jane Wright performed miracles (which I will describe in later entries) and suffered the wounds of our Lord, Jesus Christ. In the end, despite other's admonishment of her, and how she was understood as mentally incompetent, still, she continued to have her visions, and claimed to have been visited by angels and mediators, and Jesus himself. As saints are martyred and rejected, Jane too, had her share of suffering. She lived out her final years at the Mother of Mercy Home for Women, cut off from society and misunderstood. I can't say she was unhappy but more content with her situation. Even though she was abandoned by everyone, including me. Had I known what I know today, I would have stayed close to her. She suffered horribly at the hands of doctors who argued she was mentally ill. She was hospitalized a few times, given medications under close watch, as each time, she'd worsen. Eventually, her poor abused body shut down and she became catatonic. All this required increased stays in a psychiatric ward, until she was stable. I imagine it was unbearable for Jane.

And that's why I'm appealing to you, Bishop Monroe, for as a sacred man of the highest elevation, and as close to God as any mortal could get, I pray my words will evoke an emotion and compel you to act upon this injustice, for me and for my sister, Jane Wright. In all truth (pardon my presumptuousness) I can't foresee how and to what degree my words will have on you, but I desire so much for you to understand Jane, as her salvation, and mine, depend upon it, along with her daughter, Helen, whom I have raised since infanthood, and who has suffered her own share of misfortune. Helen, so sweet and docile in the early years, succumbed to addiction as a teenager, despite my support, and my devotion to her. I've always had the utmost faith in Helen and encouraged her gifts. But what we did to her, withholding the truth about her mother, perhaps, I've considered, it was unforgivable. We thought at the time it was the right thing to do, Your Excellency. I should say, it was more John who insisted upon it. God knows now I realize my error. As for my brother, John, as loyal as I am to my dear brother, Dr. Wright, I realize he was not so concerned with his own salvation. He called himself an atheist and even referred to the Bible as a mythical collection of unverifiable accounts, despite his Catholic upbringing. In his defense, we didn't attend church so regularly after our father passed away in the hurricane of 1938. I suppose Eda lost her faith, after God took her husband. John was never so keen on it, understandably so, and as a science-minded man, he has always believed Jane suffered from a mental illness, and understood her in this way, rather than as a saint, chosen by God. John was convinced she was delusional and unable to care for Helen. Fear compelled him to send her back to Mother of Mercy Home. I returned to the cottage to raise Helen. I confess, prior to the intercession of Jane, I agreed with my brother. Now I know it was a grave error on our part. Fear invokes erratic behavior, a myopic understanding, as you must know. And to think we kept Helen from the holiest of people, from a saint, a chosen savior, who we were convinced was deluded, pains me in ways I can never articulate here in this letter. We were blessed to have Mother of Mercy Home to take her in, as the sisters knew best how to tend to her in a delicate manner. They understood Jane as God's chosen one, rather than psychotic. I thank God for the sisters.

Even so, Jane was restricted and remained misunderstood by the community, and, more egregiously, by her daughter. Unfortunately, my brother John Wright passed away shortly after Jane, still steeped in doubt regarding Jane's sainthood.

As my advanced age and stiff hand prevents me from writing any further, I will continue tomorrow.

Sincerely yours in Christ,

Jennie Wright

3

1950, Jane

September 5

JOHN RETURNED EARLIER THAN expected and surprised me with lunch! We shared a sandwich and a bowl of chicken soup. I felt a calm, and even brazen. I was tempted to insist he move me to the downstairs and closer to the Sound. My mouth parted to say the words, but I stopped myself, recalling how it is not what goes in but what comes out that is defiled. Oh, how my own thoughts stultify me.

I do love him, Jennie. I do. But he tethers me, weakens me. I can barely speak in his presence. And my thoughts roam, unguarded. Before he left, he swept the floor. And I was lulled by the sound of the bristles on the wood, but when he set the broom in the closet, in my strange way, I imagined being the broom, the way he places me here or there. I imagined being placed in the closet, to rest in the quiet stillness. Am I not more than a broom? Who would deny the simplicity of a broom, unfettered, unthinking. Oh, selfish vanity, unguarded thoughts. Spare me from my secret faults and strange sins. In my final week, the baby has made me stray, mindlessly, and sapped my energies! "Get some rest," he says. "Promise me," he says. I promise. I promise. I'm at my worst,

Jennie. And John seems so sure of my situation. But I don't know that I trust him. He's confident it's hormonal, or of a physiological origin. I want to trust him. Oh Jennie. . .my soul. . .my soul is restless. I should lift up my heart, lift it up to the Lord. I so want to remember how to do it!

September 6

I could barely eat my eggs, and it worries me as the baby needs nourishment. Am I fit to be a mother? Am I selfless enough? I have no one to ask, no one to assure me. Just a faint reminder of an inner voice. No signs of John. No sounds at all. I spend an exorbitant amount of time listening for familiar creeks on the attic stairs. I sit in the nothing, waiting and waiting. I'm left disappointed and yearning for a thing, undefined. I do love him, Jennie. Why do I suspect his intentions? Maybe it's my suspicions that keep him away. Hasn't he always watched out for me? We were digging a tunnel beneath the cottage when he proposed, handed me the sterling silver ring. The tiny chip glittered. He blushed. You threw sand at us. I wore it every day, until I lost it in the Sound. But now I'm married to him! My husband, my doctor. I'm blessed, truly. Who would say that I'm not? I live in this spacious cottage on the water, married to my childhood sweetheart, my closest friend, aside from you, Jennie. And what about the ways of the destitute, the starving, the sojourner traveling for miles in a foreign place, forced out by wars and bloodshed, whereas here in the attic is spacious enough, and the air is light and plentiful, easy to breathe. And not too far below me is the Sound and the sand, endless heaps of hope, frothy foam of waves breaking, lightly, intermittently, pirouette-like. Our hideaway, Jennie. Come home!

September 7

John caught me writing. He was displeased. He frowns on my journaling. He'd rather have me knitting. "Shouldn't you be making something for the baby?" he asked. I was speechless, racked with guilt. Maybe he's right. Maybe I'm too self-indulgent. But what of the disciples, Mark and Luke and Paul and their writings? Or the blessed words of saints like Augustine, Bonaventure and Faustina? All the works I cherish. He said it again, how it's hormonal and more of a physiological origin, rather than spiritual. Is it not the doctor who is the expert in these matters? As for me, I'm unsure of my own mind, unsteady in thoughts. But what if he should force me to stop? What if? Is it for me to predict the future? I can't help but imagine it, prepare for it. I might argue with him, and go against his wishes. And then what? I couldn't stop completely. Not now. Not here in the attic, so alone with my strange thoughts. I'd become stultified, a dullard, or I'd waste the hours away, lose all sentience. Or worse, I'd remain lucid but doubt my own existence. Perhaps, then, the writing fixes me in reality. And to think, at one point, I tried to destroy all my journals. Something took hold, mid-sentence, something alien, and I decided it was wrong, and vain. It was not me but rather some incarnate deity deriving a deep satisfaction in the destruction, in watching the dyed pulp blacken and shrivel in the flames. I have confessed it many times since then. I felt myself possessed by an unseen force, and, yet, purified, transformed. You knew, somehow, Jennie. You came at me then, all arms, and wide-eyed, and ripped the journals out of my hands. Jennie, my soul, my sister, even you were alien to me.

I wonder the fate of this one. Will it outlive me? Will I destroy it, too? Will John destroy it? Taxing, he says, taxing, and, perhaps, on some level, to ponder an idea is taxing, borderline obsessive, finding the right word, delving too deeply, investing too much of one's soul in a word or a phrase.

September 8

Oh, time . . . how it ticks away. God is beyond all space and time. Oh, if I could recall a verse, some scripture on passing time. Didn't St. Augustine speak of the passing time, how past moments cease to exist but are merely a concept in our minds, and not in things.

And doesn't he discount his own words and preoccupation with these matters in his confessions? To keep one's eye solely on God taxes the mind. My own is sapped, while my senses are heightened. I sense the tide come in, the floor quake beneath me, the walls shudder. The stillness engrosses me.

I'm carrying God's heavenly gift! I should be content. I should be thankful, blessed. Instead, I'm fixating, despairing.

It was the fall, Jennie. The fall that did me in. How could God have let me slip? No one is immune. I took my eye off God, the divine. I was greedy in my actions, in a hurry to get outside to the beach, to take my morning walk, hungry for the Sound, for the misty air, the spray, the nourishment for my spirit. One slip and I went down on my back. One slip down the stairs was all it took. Now I'm forced to remain upstairs, here in the attic, and my soul thirsts for the ocean breeze, for the sand on my feet. John is convinced it's a necessary arrangement for me, and the one time in my life I should feel doted on and unfettered from daily toils and worries. I'm far enough of away from the temptation of the beach. Maybe he worries I'll walk off and never return, or get carried away by a rogue wave or lascivious stranger. He says it's best for the baby. It's only for a week or two. "Why does it bother you?" he asks me. And why should it bother me so, my submission, my resignation, my obedience, my willingness to stay here? I'm with child, with God's creation, his design, his magnificent design. We are all in God's image. And what of a minor sacrifice? Jesus spent forty days in the desert without food or drink. Saint Catherine of Siena, from the age of eight, lived on the Eucharist for twenty-five years, until her death. The martyrs gave up all earthly attachments. The saints were martyred, suffered torture and pain beyond what I can imagine.

And is it so bad in here? Once I'd loved the attic, our hideaway, Jennie, to be tucked away from the damp and sand and seas, but not too far. John reminds me. "It was your favorite place, Jane. Don't you remember? I couldn't get you two out of here." I don't say how it's changed. How it's altered over time, become more decadent. It's you, Jennie. If you were here with me, Jennie, I'd be perfectly fine, and you'd hold my hand and make me laugh, and then I wouldn't feel so far from the Sound and the sand and the jetty, which is too distant and muffled, so much so I forget where I am. You'd change it for the better. Come home, Jennie!

September 9

Intermittent pains wake me. My unguarded thoughts settle on oddities, strange proclivities. Oh, these secret faults! Oh, Lord, spare me! I consider the barnacles stuck to the rocks, satiated in their soulless state, and the crabs hiding between the rocks, then I fall into deep meditation and succumb to phantoms, envision parallel worlds, the splitting of lives, superposition, two versions of John. The John before the pregnancy. The John now. And the times before John, before the marriage, and the pregnancy, when we were unblemished, Jennie, and the sand was everything, and we buried each other's feet in the sand. I'd lift my toes and the sand cracked, like an earthquake, the tectonic plates shifting, ancient times, the reorganizing times, and the desire to bask in it, in the power of it, the small dominion, the breaking apart. We had endless time. We had time to ponder the number of mountains beneath our soft, unmarred feet, innumerable grains of sand, to suspend time, to consider the smoothing downy way about it moving over our skin.

Is it not time to put away childish things?

I try. I try.

I do love him, Jennie. I see you in him and it soothes me. I see the sand, the tides in his eyes, and when he opens the door, the smells of sea and salt, an ancient smell of wetlands, of God's creation forming, wafts over to me, saturates and fills me.

Love is complex, rightly so, a wonderment bestowed by God. I watch him when he's not aware. He takes to sitting in the wicker chair by the bookshelf, one leg folded over the other. He has a perpetual habit of lifting his chin, aiming it at the window as if to catch the sun. A beam of sunlight touches the top of his head and the side of his face. And his hands. . .oh, how adorable his hands, the way he moves one so deftly along the spine of books, pausing, now, as if a bird as caught his eye, or some soaring spectacle. It's as if he's trapped within himself, his soul crying for release, the old John, the one I long for now. My mind screams out, How long will you stay with me, John? How long will I wait for your return?

September 10

I rescind my earlier comments! I repent! Forgive me! Give me fire to burn these words, these unholy pages! Oh, the doubt that depletes me, wears at my soul! It's John, all John, sustaining me with just a light touch and cool lips pressed against mine. And his hand, ah, the healing hand that mends and revives so many dying hearts and minds. I ached to grab his hand, to keep him, and he intuited my insatiable need, and he said, I love you, Jane, and he said it, what I suspected all along, how he's saddened and worried, very worried. He says I'm taxed. He's right. I'm depleted, worn, wasted. I assured him I'm fine. But then he patted my stomach, and I caught it, the furrowed brow, and I'm troubled . . . intensely troubled.

4

Jennie, 2020

Re: Jane's Torments

Most Reverend Sir,

I am well rested and by the Grace of God ready to continue my thoughts on the canonization of Jane Wright.

I'm so blessed to wake each day. After morning toast and a walk in the garden, amidst the hydrangeas and lilies and roses, and then to the shoreline, close to the breaking waves. Ah! The spray of sea, God's divine anointing, and I feel rejuvenated, as if my Jane is walking alongside me in approval. And now I shift to a darker tone, a sadder one, when I think of my Jane, how she was in the attic, alone, cut off from her beloved beach, how she must have suffered. But Maribel is uplifting as she is so good to me, Your Excellency, and I do wish I could repay her for all she's done for us. She walks with me, holds my arm and keeps me steady. Despite Jane's mistrust of her, as I find in her entries, Maribel is in no way cruel, but the kindest of souls, and did the best she could for Jane, under the circumstances. We were both unsure, beside ourselves, and so we conferred with the professional, who happened to be my brother, Dr. Wright.

Jane suffered greatly from a very young age, and she was ostracized for her beliefs, and all the while, she was better than most, and she suffered for us, for our Godly parts, for our good, for humanity. She never asked to be chosen, to be exulted as a healer. Once, she said to me, "I never asked for this, you know." She was teary-eyed, struggling. My poor, poor Jane. I don't know that I could have handled it. Either way, I endeavor to provide you with the full account of Jane. Although I can't decipher the degree of her fears, I believe she was both at peace and tormented.

What I can do is to reflect back to those times, to find some inkling of what was to come. During our stays at the beach, we shared the same bedroom, as I mentioned. I was close in all manners of closeness and imbibed her tumult. The two of us were like twins in that we had a profound connection, and I'd say we knew each other's thoughts. Still, no matter how close, it was never enough. I yearned for more understanding, for more wisdom when it came to Jane. I fell short, always, and remained on the perimeter of Jane's life, an observer, and for this reason I'm not able to provide an exact account of what she experienced. One can only presume to conjecture on another's mind. But I suspect Jane is here with me, next to me, guiding me, incarnating me, working through me to write this letter. I can tell you what was described to me in Jane's words. I can describe what I witnessed, and what she said, how it felt to exist in the outer realms. I can share her words. Let me just say, I would add, it isn't what you think or imagine it to be. But then again, maybe you, as the Bishop, revered and closer to God, have experience with these matters yourself. Maybe that's what brought you to devote your waking hours to God. Jane told me on her dying bed, how it was so much more than I could imagine. Her eyes lit up, illuminated against a pitch-black evening, a storm raging outside the Mother of Mercy Home. Don't get me wrong, my poor Jane, she suffered for it, especially towards the end. She cried out for her daughter, Helen, and this is the sole purpose I write to you, Your Excellency, to give an honest account of Jane Wright, and argue her case, why she deserves to be ordained as a saint, prayed to, and exulted for the devotees who pray to her, still. This highest honor, if bestowed upon Jane, is just the right kind of justice and reverence she, and her darling daughter, Helen, deserve.

Imagine, if you will, Bishop Monroe, how a mother, lucid and deeply sensitive, must feel to be in this circumstance, ostracized, forbidden to see her baby, and discouraged to read and write, which was truly the only outlet for her, the only way Jane knew to process the events that occurred within her and outside of her. She was of a sensitive nature and swallowed her world up so completely. I imagine Jane attempting to write with constraint and shame. It would bring any sane mother to the brink of insanity. Then again, in defense of my brother, Dr. John Wright, and his actions, how could he have thought otherwise? I know a heart heartened is difficult to soften.

Your Reverence, if you haven't imbibed my passion, yet, let me assure you, I write to you trembling, barely able to contain my emotions, my genuine devotion for Jane, with her voice in my head, with her hand on mine. And whether it comes from Jane's spirit, well, that cannot be proven, definitively, but merely felt, as in the Holy Spirit sense. Let me say, Your Reverence, I am convinced of ethereal currents of energy, these matters occurring in life, deemed unquantifiable, not because they can't be measured, but due more to the fact that we don't believe they require the application of a calculation. And herein lies the crux. Although Jane has passed on to the Eternal Kingdom, her energies should not be dismissed, but rather weighed and calculated. And Helen should know her mother's true nature, her true essence, that she was not psychotic or disturbed but rather highly sensitive to the fourth dimension, or the outer realms beyond our earthly understanding. Only then will Helen truly thrive and turn her eyes to God.

If you will, Bishop Monroe, I beg you to examine the evidence, carefully, and with an open mind. Please consider Jane's journal entries, the witnesses, the doctor notes, all of which I've included. Who knew she needed me so much? I can't describe the despondence I experienced after reading her journals. At the time, I was not available to her and was, instead, selfishly sailing to remote islands with my fiancé Maxwell. In the end, I suffered for it. Maxwell was a deceitful man, not of a Godly nature. It was all manipulation and lasciviousness. Still, I forgive him for his ways. He was raised in an ungodly home. As for me, I was weak, enamored, driven by lust, by flesh, by earthly matters, and by the richness of the life, the carnality of it, the lushness of the islands and customs, so much so I neglected my sister, my soul, my best friend. I never knew until it was too late, when I was summoned by John to the cottage. She was gone. All I had were her journals, what was left of them, and I was compelled to read them. At one point, between hospitalizations, she had lost her sense of reality and proceeded to tear each page out and rip it into tiny shreds. I caught her at the fireplace tossing in pages, and her eyes were dark and foreign, staring into the flames. I stopped her and I was able to salvage some entries. Here, in these entries is evidence of Jane's conflict, the turbulence inside her mind, the ancient battle between the purest and most vile of human nature. As you must know, the holier one becomes, the more susceptible to the evil and temptation. I wonder, Your Reverence, if you have had your own share of inner battles. Parden me for mentioning, but you are mortal, after all, and aren't we all subject to carnality? We all seek ways to discern the good from the evil. Jane, however, was a frail creature, as so many younger saints proved to be. She had no support from her fellow creatures who believed her to be deluded, or monstrous, and some even suggested she was an addict. I'd say they were right, in that regard, as she was addicted to God and to her faith. So many are addicted to worldly things, and share a myopic understanding of life, their existence, their purpose.

My eyes are strained today, Your Reverence, so I will continue tomorrow with the first miracle, which I'd intended to get to today.

Your loyal servant in Christ,

Jennie Wright

5

Jane, 1950

September 11

OH, JENNIE! I TRIED to sleep, but a dark pall compassed me! How does one fall so horribly? Once I was washed clean and pure. Now I'm rooted, bedridden, pained, breathless, all carnality. What else can I say? If I describe it otherwise, I'd be deceitful. It's become worse. If I dare fall asleep, I wake soaked, trembling from foreign entities. Dark shapes, serpentine and ungodly, swirl and dance about me. I want to believe it's a holy divination, a testing of sorts commissioned by God. Please, I pray, let it be! But if it were his doings, why should I be so unsettled? How long? How long? Even outside . . . below me the waves are a watery rage, breaking in fitful ways. And I wait for sunrise, for the tides to turn, for the lull. I wait an interminable amount of time, while the tumult persists, and persists, and then morphs in my imaginings, and it is no longer the tide and breaking waves but something else, a plane, perhaps, plummeting, bellowing, the hollow sound of descent, a whale's cry as it careens downward, a sinister leviathan, a metal bird aimed at the attic, predatorily, intending to seer off the top of the cottage, taking the attic in its talons. And to think once the Sound was music, pacifying, lulling me to blissful sleep—all trickery! I try and try to turn away from the fecundity, from the slosh and the mire of temptation, the lustful and maligned, and well I should. I will my eyes upward to the beams above me, to escape the steamy vapors; the marsh moans in protest, moans and wails like souls stewing and bubbling up to the surface, and I gasp for air, my mouth opening in a silent howl, an eternal agony affixing to my face.

Outside, the wind whips furiously against the mad rush of water. All I can do is pray, Jennie, in the few words I recall. Oh, merciful God, free me from the wiles of my enemies, from those who seek to ruin my soul! Send my Jennie home to me! Amen.

September 12

The sun is foreign, ungraspable. The dimness fills my days. You'd free me, Jennie. You'd free me from this insufferable torment. You'd insist I be moved downstairs. I know you, Jennie, like I know my own soul. Like Mary to Jesus, that's how you were with John. I've never been more certain of a thing. How is it that I am in this attic? Why? What is it about me that obeys so willingly, submits to unreasonable demands? Just one slip on the stairs, and I'm trapped, imprisoned, and I agree to such demands, as if I'd lost lucidity. If I were to weigh the situation, I'd call it unjust, lacking in proportionality. As I write, Jennie, I feel the blood rushing to my cheeks, an anger untapped, stewing.

I'm unhinged when I should submit to discomforts, for the sake of the baby, take up my cross and carry it. I should be pure and virtuous. I should remember Evan Ward, unable to walk, or partake, but gracious just to watch the waves, the boats, smell the sea, His father would wheel him outside. He'd pick him up like a baby and place him on a towel.

"Go ahead," John mocked me. "Go ahead and heal him," he'd said, because of my resurrection, and because I healed Eda and Melissa Haighworth, and because of the visitors who came to the cottage to see me, to touch me, to pray with me, so I might heal them. John was envious, maybe, and mistrustful, said I was feeding other's delusions. I went with my heart, submitted to my inner voice, and not because he goaded me. I followed my soul's voice. John said it was idolatrous to pray to saints, to worship someone other than God. I was speechless, initially. But God spoke for me, armed me with words, helped me to explain how all believers have the Holy Spirit in their hearts, so just as Jesus interceded on our behalf, we, too, should intercede for one another. You were so incensed with your brother for the way he goaded me, but I forgave him. I still forgive him. I kept it to myself, the way my soul spoke to me and advised me. We don't always know God's plan. I sat beside Evan and prayed. I kept these things in my heart. By the end of the summer, Evan walked! John dismissed it as a coincidence. I doubted, too, initially, but my soul's inner voice was relentless. Maybe it was Faustina who interceded on my behalf. I'd immersed myself in her diary, and I'd felt a profound devotion to her. She, too, was fallible, unsure, resistant to her inner voice. Eventually, she submitted. I did the same and sat beside Evan Ward. And it was really no trouble at all. I prayed for him, a novena for healing. And by the end of the summer, not only could he walk, but Evan Ward went on to become a Rhodes Scholar and renown author, and I'm mentioned in his book. "Nothing shy of a miracle," he'd said regarding the healing. I didn't talk about it to him or anyone, how I prayed to the venerated St. Philomena and Padre Pio and St. Faustina, and other intercessors for healing. When Evan was outside, no matter what was going on, I remained close to him and held his hand, and I prayed for his healing. He accepted it and prayed with me. I don't take any credit. I was merely an instrument of God's mercy. It was so easy to understand back then. God manifested in me and I was able to show signs of his mercy and great glory.

No more, Jennie. I'm not the same person. It's as if I've been reborn into a new flesh, unholy and unworthy, greedy and wanting. Maybe God discarded me. I've lost all virtuosity. I'm fallen, distracted by earthly desires. I struggle to recapture it, the stirring presence of the divine sifting through my tarnished soul and waiting for acceptance. I accept! I accept!

6

Jennie, 2020

Re: Summers with Jane

Dear Bishop Monroe,

I am so blessed to be alive, to wake to another day! Despite the inclement weather, I'm elated!

I feel as if nothing can dampen my spirits, dissuade me from completing my correspondence to you. It's of no significance, the dark clouds, the encroaching storm. All stymies me, the fickle ways of nature so much like people, the way we love in one moment and loath in the next. I've never carried a child, so I can't fathom the anxieties exacerbated by an active imagination such as Jane's. These times, as I write to you, I feel Jane is with me, most profoundly, and it conjures up one of our favorite scenes from *Wuthering Heights* and Catherine's famous line, "I am Heathcliff." We'd hang on these words, say it in unison, clutch hands, cry, laugh. That is how I feel about Jane, although certainly not in any sort of desirous manner, but more in a sharing of spirit, of kinship.

I can't help but notice, Your Reverence, the dark skies and such an abominably abysmal day, and to think just a short time ago the cardinal perched, peacefully, on the tip of the branch, and the sun played off the tips of the leaves, speckled the ground to an artist's delight. And now the rain is hard and slanted and pummels the roof and the tops of the trees. My hand is steady, surprisingly, and I feel God is with me, guiding it along these pages. My heart swells. I can barely keep a dry eye. And I suppose, yes, I suppose, I should be thankful for the dampened earth and replenishing. Jane always loved the rain and would dash out into it, singing and spinning, whereas John was more apt to take shelter and remain until a clearing. The two were polar opposites, now that I consider it. In all fairness to my dear brother, I've never known a person like Jane, and I suspect I never will. I imagine she must have been difficult to decipher at times. Ours was not the average relationship. Still, I had the advantage. Understand, Your Reverence, I knew Jane long before my brother John married her. As I might have mentioned in a previous entry, our mothers shared a dorm at Ratcliffe. The two were inseparable, like sisters, Eda had said. Ruth, Jane's mother, always stayed for a few weeks, and then returned to Maryland, but Jane stayed for the entire summer. If you can imagine it, Your Reverence, a brown shingled cottage at the end of a cul-de-sac, by no means modest, but certainly no mansion. Built in 1929 by my father, Taylor Wright, a doctor and boatsman, for his first wife, Suzette, who loved the ocean and wanted to remain close to her parents in Old Lyme. Suzette died shortly after their wedding. A year later, my father met my mother, Eda, at a café in Soundview. They married and had John and then me.

Ours was one of the first cottages on Shoreline Drive, before the smaller rainbow cottages were built, a time when there was vast open spaces, blueberry bushes and marsh, and the gypsies came to the shore in caravans and gathered mussels and barnacles from the jetties and scoped the marshes for beavers and otters and turtles and frogs, for sustenance and potions and pelts.

It was during these times that Jane stayed the summer, when we grew closer, and I observed her idiosyncratic ways. I merely accepted her as children do, even the most outrageous things. In fact, some of what I will disclose will be difficult to write in recollection of it, and maybe even for Your Reverence to bear, and, for this reason, I've kept silent. As it is now, most who have encountered

Jane understood her wrongly. I can't count the number of times Jane has been assaulted, cast off, abandoned, criminalized, referred to as psychotic, deluded, possessed. The only safe place for her was in the confines of Mother of Mercy Home. And even that home wasn't entirely safe, after an attempted arson by extremists who believed Jane Wright was an apostate angel returned to earth, who needed to be destroyed. Isn't it true most saints suffered similar fates? And our poor courageous savior himself, our Lord Jesus Christ, suffered the worst, and all for us.

I will explain thoroughly why these accusers were misguided, and why I hold no ill will towards the skeptics, knowing they were victims of a secular society too rapt in the modern day to understand divinity, or a true reverence in physical form. And I forgive them because it was Jane who taught me to reject earthly nuisances, and that anger merely begets anger. Jane forgave her enemies. Jane was blessed with extraordinary wisdom, like that of Solomon. And in ways much truer. We are fallen creatures. All of us floundering, blindly. Even he, yes, even King Solomon succumbed to hubris and sinned against God. The weight of his gold amounted to the number of the beast. Coincidence? One can desire too much.

Your Excellency, I hope you will pardon me for presuming to know Jane's motives. If she were alive, as we were so indistinguishable, she might be writing these very same words, in praise of someone else, of course. Jane was self-effacing and humble. I assure you, I was her confidante in no uncertain terms, and she mine. Prior to Maxwell, Jane was my study. I followed Jane closely and listened intently to her words. I was convinced they came from a higher power—God, himself. She turned my eyes to God. I've been warned of my own dire circumstances, due to disbelief for so long. Now my purpose to forgive my enemies is twofold: I want to exult myself to the highest degree, lose all bitterness, all the resentment and anger Jane worked so hard to dismiss, knowing if left unchecked how it seeps into one's soul.

But enough of me. I'm prepared for more of it, more skeptics, more backlash. I've kept quiet for too long. Now I'm unencumbered and alone, and I disclose the full story of Jane Wright, my dear, loving friend; I don't expect anyone to believe me. They will turn on me, as they turned on her so frequently. Perhaps they will attempt to silence me, to cancel me, to commit me. And now it won't matter. No, not at my advanced age. And I won't blame them. I barely believe it myself.

It is no surprise, I am suddenly now overwrought and heated. Maribel, such a kind woman, she's brought me my evening tea, and so, once again, I'll have to resume tomorrow with Jane's first miracle.

Until then,
Jennie Wright

7

Jane, 1950

September 14

HOW LONG BEFORE I see the sun? How long must I wait? A dark cloud settles over the cottage. Oh, Jennie. If only I had better news to share. But I've fallen into shame and abominations. My soul thirsts for the sensual. I try and try, but I barely remember how to pray, as I've forgotten the words. My soul is still and silent. I'm ill, sick with a strange sadness, burdened with aches and pains not attributed to the pregnancy. Although John would beg to differ. He doesn't know the pain I feel. He can't ever know. My soul is depleted. I know these are trials, but there is a chance I may never return to my previous state. I'd be so much healthier if you were here, and if I were free from these constraints. I should trust him, my husband. He's your brother, and my closest ally, but my back is healed. Still, he insists, in his stubborn way, I remain in the attic.

Jennie, come to me! I'm overwrought! My soul languishes! I sense a darkness pervading my soul!

September 15

Oh what a sun can do for a soul, a light for the forlorn ailing soul. John was so thoughtful as to install the stained glass in the gable window. Now it's a kaleidoscope of colors, a bountiful hope. And these times, St John's words return to me, how love is not tried by ease and satisfaction. The conflicts we endure, the cross we carry, is in no measure equal to our Lord and Savior, our sweet and merciful Emmanuel. How good it feels to write these words, as if my hand were guided by an incarnate deity, my soul washed. Am I returning? Oh what a merciful God!

I should confess my greed, my yearning, my desire for more, for the Sound and the feel of the sand on my feet, for the salty air, for my freedom. Do I dare? Once I went up and down the stairs, unrestricted. I took long walks on the beach. I'm healed more than ever before and in all manners of speaking.

But how to convince John? I could explain to him how the attic is changed, how it discomfits me, how it taunts me.

If only you were here, Jennie. You'd make him do it, or you'd be my voice, you'd arm me, make me say the words, like Aaron spoke for Moses. What can I do but pray. God, if it be your will, send Jennie to me. And if not, please grant me the patience to endure my trials and find comfort in the divine creation. All by your hand, God. Amen.

8

Jennie, 2020

Re: First Miracle

Dear Bishop Monroe,

I can't tell you what it's like to wake to the ebbing tide, and the smells of the Sound. Now with Helen moved away, and Eda long gone, and John and Jane deceased, the sea has been my companion for some years now. I never liked being alone and even shared a bedroom with John. It made me feel safer to have him with me. When Jane returned for the summers, John would retreat to his room, a bit sullen, so I imagined. It left me conflicted, so happy to have my lovely Jane back, but sorry for John. We lost our father at a young age, as I mentioned earlier. Our father's boat capsized in the hurricane of 1938. I was only eight-years old. They never retrieved Taylor Wright. Parts of his Port Carling Seabird washed up on shore for years after. In fact, each time we found a piece of mahogany wood, we'd claim it. Eda was left raise us with the help of our nanny, Maribel, who still lives here at the cottage.

Whenever I look at the few pictures we have of Taylor Wright, even to this day, I try to imagine him, examine his tall person, study him from head to toe, seeking a semblance to us, or to tap into some small memory of him—his laugh or his smell. I can fairly say, I have little recollection of him. Eda, as we referred to her, our mother, could hardly utter his name without tearing up. I'm ashamed to say, I envied her for knowing him so well, and being so distraught she couldn't bear to tell us much about him. She'd say he was a good man with a giant heart who lived for the sea. Although he was a doctor, he quit his practice to spend more time sailing. He refurbished sailboats, too, and new all there was to know about them. I remember how he'd bounce me on one knee and John on the other and tell us stories about his boating adventures, fishing, storms, his close encounters with death, and ghosts. According to our father, the seas were haunted.

Now that I've provided a bit of context, Your Reverent Sir, I'll begin with the first miracle, which begins with a séance.

We'd been on the beach, per usual, and the sun was on its final descent. The sky was crimson and created an effervescent glow on the water. Our favorite cousins were visiting, Bernice and Benjamin. The twins both shared the same hair, freckles, gestures, and manner of talking. And they did just about anything we asked them to do. It was my idea to have a séance and bring back our father, now gone for two years. We were of the same age, the same mind, the three of us. Jane, on the other hand, pleaded for us to stop, partly because she too had lost her father, recently, to a heart malady. John took her side. He had a special fondness for Jane, even when we were young, and he took her side in all matters. He was the logical one, whereas I was more lured to the supernatural. Jane waffled back and forth and was fearful of ghosts and dark shadows, things that go bump in the night, so to speak. When father told ghost stories, especially the one about the vile pirate, Gunder, wielding a giant fishhook, seeking vengeance of past ills, I'd have to read Jane uplifting stories to lull her to sleep, and even the Sound didn't suffice. High tide coming in sent Jane's sensitive nature into a tailspin. She'd assign emotions to the Sound, referring to it as angry or possessed or lonely. I decided her frame of mind was manifested in the waves.

I recall the waves that night were unusually rough. Each time one broke we'd be sprayed, and the candle went out, and we'd burst out in feigned anger and hysteria, fists raised and aimed at father's water ghosts, as if we could outdo the Atlantic in our youthful mindset. I suppose, in hindsight, I can say we liked to place ourselves in these risky circumstances. All too soon, and matured, we're apt to apply logic to all situations, and our senses are dulled to a certain degree, in order to avoid risk at all costs. In other words, once aged and seasoned, our lives become controlled and predictable. Your Excellency, please forgive me for going off on yet another tangent, as I'm inclined to do. I can't help but imagine what you're contemplating as you read my words, wondering if I will ever get to the point. But you see, all I write is essential to a full understanding of Jane and why we didn't watch her more carefully that night. We were naïve, indestructible, and, therefore, blameless. Points about Jane spill out, unprovoked, spontaneously, and I feel she has a part in this digression, and it's all purposeful. Jane spoke so much of her inner voice being her soul's voice, I feel Jane is just that, guiding my hand along the page.

Suffice it to say, I'm not quite certain where my words are taking me. But I have a strange confidence in them, as if they are operating outside my consciousness, and I've tapped into some other realm, one you're closer to, Your Reverence. Jane has always had a way of guiding a person to enlightenment without their awareness.

But now, once again, as time has gotten away from me, Maribel, my lovely friend, she's just knocked on my door and I'm forced to return to this grand undertaking tomorrow morning. The rain is beating, mercilessly, on the roof, and windowpanes, and I hear the wind picking up. It will be an unsettled night tonight, and it doesn't help that I've gone and conjured up Gunder and other bad spirits. I can hear Jane's admonishments.

Until tomorrow.

Yours in Christ,

Jennie Wright

Re: First Miracle continued . . .

Dear Bishop Monroe,

I do hope and pray your morning is as lovely as mine. No blessing is as sharp as when a storm subsides. What a miraculous way the earth regenerates. From outside my window, there is the morning light hitting the tips of our chestnut tree. And if that weren't magical enough, a cardinal perches on the very tip of the branch. I believe it's a sign, my dear Jane paying me a visit, maybe in support of my writing. I feel the environment induces the most profound reflections. I am almost ashamed to have such a pleasant alcove where my desk sits with a window facing the east, and one off to the side of the room facing the west, so I'm blessed to catch a rising sun in the morning, hitting the chestnut tree, and one vibrant and visceral setting at night.

But I digress. As I mentioned, in my previous entry, during the séance, the waves were breaking and spraying us, and the candle kept going out, and we were chanting some random words to summon up Taylor Wright, holding hands, requesting his presence, and at some point, I can't say exactly when, we lost sight of Jane. I decided she may have crept inside to get away from the dark. I was satisfied with that theory, but John insisted we look for her. So after a bit of time passed, when I was convinced father wasn't coming, I went inside and called out to her. When there was no reply, and the cottage was thoroughly searched, we returned to the beach. Some time passed, maybe an hour or so, and Eda had joined the search party, and suggested we call the police. And that's about the time we heard Benjamin shouting, "Over here!" He was standing on the jetty at the creek, about five-hundred feet or so from our cottage. We rushed to him, feet slipping in the sand, hearts racing, lost in our childish and fantastical thinking, adrenaline pumping. While I'm sure the adults were fearing the worst. Jane was known to have spells where she'd wander off, aimlessly, and seem to lose all awareness as if she were sleepwalking. As I got closer, it dawned on me, the reality of the situation. I prayed she was safe, but when I peered down below, my heart just about stopped. Below in the dark waters, illuminated, slightly, by either a possible moon glow, or the LED spotlights from the cottage, it was just enough light to reveal our sweet Jane floating in the icy cold grips of the creek. To see her like that. . .oh, the horror of it! It's an image I can't forget, Your Reverence. Her pretty long brown hair I'd liked to braid and brush, now splayed out in the murky, black depths. I only wish I could convey the intensity of the moment. I'm afraid my words fail me. My life, my heart, my soul, my Jane—I sensed she was dead. John dove in and pulled her up onto our favorite rock, the pretty pink granite. How many times had we stretched out on that very rock to dream, or pop caps, or sing songs, or to dry off after a swim.

John commenced CPR, and we were distraught. "What did you do?" John said, as if our Jane did it intentionally. Eda was touching her face, moving her hair to the side, copious tears running down her cheeks. At some point, the ambulance had arrived and the paramedics took over, and we felt the urgency, heard the dire words, "No pulse," in quiet utterances, and even the water once breaking on the rocks, now calmed, and the air grew still and somber. Those two words, *no pulse*, reverberated off the rocks, lingered above me, planted into my psyche, to return and haunt me. "No, she can't be!" John cried out, and "Save her! Dear God, save her!" My dear brother was beside himself. A skeptic and unbeliever, John was now begging God to save Jane. Admittedly, I was numb, immobile, unable to utter a word. Jane, my soul, she lay there on the rocky ravine, limp, unreal, and without a pulse for almost half an hour, which seemed like a lifetime. I felt then as if I could die right along with her.

But here is where the atmosphere shifts, Your Reverence. Just when the situation seemed most dire and hopeless, a strange new kind of light in the black of the night, a light so bright we had to squint, appeared out of nowhere. I had initially believed it was a flashlight from one of the paramedics. One might have considered an alien ship beaming down on us from above, or a helicopter, except there was no sound at all, aside from John's cries of relief, as our dear Jane was alive! The paramedics were stymied, as now

Jane, who was without a pulse and for all intents and purposes deceased, was sitting up and rubbing her eyes and very much alive.

I'll end on that note, with the first miracle fresh in my mind, Reverent Sir, as Maribel is here now to take me to my appointment.

Sincerely yours in Christ,

Jennie Wright

9

Jane, 1950

September 17

ALMOST TWO WEEKS HAVE passed. Each time I hear the creak on the stairs, I imagine it's you, Jennie. I'm still here. The baby still kicks. The foghorn still bellows, except it's not like you'd remember. I find it odder, a strangely peculiar sound, a long, slow cry, as if to ask, *where,* in a new voice, lifeless, flat against the thick grass. And the silence, afterwards, is forlorn.

Time is endless, incalculable in this attic. My mind conjures up the marsh, the tall cordgrass entangling me until it binds my mind, my hands, my feet. Beyond the marsh and grass is a dense fog. Directly in front is the tall cordgrass, swaying, as if parted by a creature of ungodly stature and gait. I'm at battle with the darker powers.

Now it's John at the door, and the howling wind, the piercing pain, the crack of old wood and glass panes.

Update . . .

I asked about the nursery. John said, "It's lovely, Jane." I should go. I should go. You'd take me. I envision us, Jennie, the descent, my body wracked and reeling, the creak of the stairs, traversing the labyrinth-like space, your encouraging words. He sat in the wicker chair, chin pointed upwards, reticent. We both wait for the event.

John assured me a few more days. I rubbed my stomach, felt a tiny heel kick my side, and it dawned on me, soon enough I'll be pushing this life out of me, the flesh and bones, the sinew, the screams, the blast of atoms. I want to be far from myself, far from here, from this attic, to find new air. Even you knew it was best to move away. And John, even he likes to be away, too.

But he tried. He tried to make it brighter, added a fresh coat of paint along the molding, hung a painting of Matisse. But the small patch of wallpaper next to the bookshelf, just that one spot, it taunts me with its sickly pall, the faded, stale yellow with its creepy crawling ivy, and other lines creating indiscernible patterns and shapes. A soul aches for symmetry. I should suffer the ills of others. I should suffer the torments like the Passion. I should delve into the pattern, into the swelling yellow and swim in the madness. With each jolt of pain, it seems to intensify, enlarge itself on my retinas, weave here and there, infinitely, in a sort of forlorn and lost way. I know too well the despair of the wallpaper. In an attempt to quell the darkness, I imagine you with Maxwell, assuaged by the tides. And to think, you were the one to notice the wallpaper. You were compelled to pick at it, to peel it, whenever we were plotting or dreaming. We were naïve, unsuspecting.

Oh, Lord, my Father, I lament on how a place can change in gruesome ways. Where once it was a refuge from storms and sand and sea, our blessed hideaway, a respite from the relentless scratch of sand and shells, the rough weather and crash of waves, the grating sneers of adults. John always came for us. And the look in his eyes, envy, and something else. I still wait for John. I wait and wait. The wallpaper knows, as if it's sentient. Protect me. Arm me.

Now the pain again. It's time. Like he says, almost time, Jane. I don't like his eyes when he says, almost time.

September 18

All by his hand and his alone. Trouble comes to those who stray in their thoughts. I knew it once as an absolute. But now I've changed and became doubtful, distracted, and I think less of those matters. I pray it's true, what I suspect, that God is present and is warning me, testing me with trials, kindling up envy and angst and an unsettled distraction, and at least it's some consolation, even if I can't proclaim it. John discourages me in those regards. Perhaps it's a fear of losing me. He wants me logical, present, evenly raked like the sand in the morning. John is a clairvoyant. He is too aware, too keen. I see worry in his downcast eyes, his brow, his pallor. I wonder why I should worry him so.

But I'm here in the attic. Does he care that I'm alone? Indifference is the worst treatment. Am I invisible? Does he see me? Am I more than a broom to be set here and there? I suffer like a restless spirit lingering in a past world. My soul aches for past desires, for a John I knew in a different universe, when we laughed and played, when the stars glittered and time was irrelevant.

Jennie! Where are you? I pray these words reach across the sea and grab hold of your soul! The wallpaper hangs in strips, hangs like peeling flesh, worse than I recall, dingier from decades of dank air. How could he? How could he leave me alone so long? All is outdone by it, Jennie. All is undone by the decadence of the wallpaper. It's peeling more aggressively, hanging more horridly. After the newspaper article, in another time, they came to me, wanting to be healed. Who was I then, Jennie? Who am I now? I've altered, and now I'm impure, ungodly in my thoughts. The paper knows. It mocks me like the bullies who circled me, shouted obscenities at me, called me a witch, a sorcerer, saved their fruit and other items from lunch to throw at me. Eventually, I stopped going to school. Those times were hard for me, Jennie, harder than now. I should be content, thankful and praising.

But the paper . . . Why is it still here? After all those years. I should walk right up to it and rip it off, one tear, one swipe. But then what? John left it for a reason. Maybe to distract me from myself, to remind me of my iniquities and pains. I should be thankful.

1 a.m.

I'm trembling. The paper haunts my sleep. I shudder to close my eyes. The unborn screams to be born. I'm dramatic, I know, Jennie. I'm overwrought, overcome by waves of pain. I freeze, lest I move and it stops my breath, my heart, and ends me. If only I could tell you, Jennie. I can barely write the words. It's a good pain. I should be brave like the women before me, like our Divine Mother, Mary. But I need you!

Why do you stay away from me? You're my confessor, my confidante. I yearn to tell you. My body and soul aches.

They say I'll give birth any day now, God's creature, and all I desire is our raft, the soft play of the Sound against it, the whistle of air from our noses, the soft breaths, and I'd confess to you now, if I could, how alone, how scared, the fear I have for the baby inside me, and, oh, how it loathes me, kicks me, fiercely, sharply, as if it detests its prison-like womb.

September 20

Oh, Jennie! I can hear you in my head, so clearly now, my counsel, my spirit, saying chin up, Jane, and you have John, and he loves you. Yes, I'm sure of it. He does care. I can tell in the way he tends to me, worries about me, and gives me a pill or two for sleep. I resist closing my eyes, where once I'd craved it. I rather like to stay awake, imagine you in a swirl of aquamarine waters, the South Pacific, the Galapagos and Easter Island, exotic places, the shimmer of colors, the trillions of coral and sea creatures of magnificent form, ones I can't now define, and the glow of a purer sun than mine. My waters are murky, darker, colder. We wanted so badly to see our feet, remember? Do you think of me? I took two white pills, and now I'm lax and sluggish, and soon enough I'll return, against my wishes, to sleep, to the marsh and mire.

September 21

I wish so much to return, Jennie, to be renewed. I say nothing. I keep all things in my heart. A misunderstanding can lead to the unthinkable. Faustina had a proper confessor, one who understood her, the complexities of God's plans. Even Faustina was understood as deluded. Even she was told she was not saintly enough for God's visions. I want to be renewed, returned to my previous state. For now, I dwell in chaos, in the careless stream of consciousness that is ungodly and vain. I suffer the torments of self-inflicted doubt. The baby kicks and jars me back, and I can't help but imagine, in these mysteriously dark places, the fetus fearing an ungodly womb, imbibing my ghastly fears. I am weighed down by gross iniquities, perplexed by my anxieties, unwound, knowing I should be something else, knowing I should be awestruck, paralyzed with love and devotion of a nurturing kind, of God's divine working inside of me. If only I could destroy the wallpaper, the negative energies waxing about me. How can I imagine myself an empty vessel, when my womb is blessed, filled with God's greatest design? My soul aches for forgiveness, for purity, for the Holy Spirit. It can only be that I've lost touch with the divine, where once I was chosen, washed clean. I've turned away. A dark pall lingers and compasses me. I was someone else back then. After my resurrection, I was changed, not of this earth. No more. No more. Now I've been cast down like an apostate, all carnality. I can't help but think they were right, the ones who sought to pummel me, to imprison me, to drug me. Maybe they were right. Maybe I'm where I deserve.

A sharp kick. I gasp for air. Why me, Jennie? Why? Part of me wants to disintegrate, turn to dust and blow away in the wind. It whips in fury against the mad rush of sea. Make haste. Come to me, Jennie! Oh, merciful God, free me from the wiles of my enemies, from those who seek to ruin my soul! Amen.

Update . . .

2:00 a.m.

I woke from a dream, Jennie. It returned to me . . . my resurrection. I was changed, newly washed, made clean and pure.

And I thought to myself, what have I done to deserve this? Why? How did I know? My inner soul replied to me, and I knew it was my path. All things paled in comparison. My world grew bigger, brighter, more vivid, and realer. God's messenger visited me in my sleep. I'm sure of it, and reminded me of my soul's new desire. I was transformed, became prescient, and I knew without knowing. But who could prove themselves worthy of such a calling? Who? Me? I'd be afraid of me. You were afraid of me, Jennie. I worried for you, for sinners, for their salvation, for the unbelievers who rejected me, loathed me, refused to accept my message and the resurrection of Jesus. Even at ten-years old, I knew all this. You were afraid. You studied me, as if I were a curious specimen. When I moved, even slightly, you watched me. When I spoke, you fixed on my mouth, questioned what I said and why. If I were to raise my arm, you followed it. If I gazed outward in thought, you did the same. As if emulating me might offer some insight into the new me. You puzzled over me. All my parts, once so familiar and comfortable to you, were alien. And it was all because of the change, the time I went to a place beyond this world, beyond what others can only imagine, and I had a vision. And it returned to me in my dream. I'd forgotten. Now I remember. The light and eyes and wings stretched out across the sky and colors of ember and sapphire, leaving trails of energies, this seraph moved back and forth, and up and down, and all ways, and said, "You will be saved to save others." And in short time, I was awakened, looking up at you, Jennie, and John and the others, with the smell and taste of briny water in my nostrils and throat.

Maybe I should have died in the creek, I'd thought. Why me, God? Why did I have to witness the sins of our humanity, the prophesy of pain and bloodshed, there in the icy cold of the creek? I was only ten-years old, Jennie. So young. How will I ever save anyone? I was afraid of my soul, even of you, Jennie.

At the Mother of Mercy Home, I was embraced, empowered, armed with faith, a new shield, no longer committee to that of earthly pleasures but to the spiritual realm, to my one and only Father, the God of Abraham and Isaac and Jacob. I was a crucial part of the covenant. John wrote to me, daily, tried to convince me to come home, to marry him, but I was unable to see beyond a profound love for Jesus and a devotion to God, my one and only Father. As my studies finished, and my eighteenth birthday approached, I had to make a choice, to stay on with the sisters, or return home. I suffered from indecision. I couldn't imagine my life away from it, from my sisters. The notion of devotion to anyone but God was unfathomable. I knew if I chose earthly possessions, I'd lose my place in his eyes. I feared becoming misplaced, confused, unable to find my way back.

I consider it all, my divine purpose, how many I've healed, but even when I consider it, I feel resistant to it, too much of myself, too attached, too fearful of losing my corporality, drifting off, losing you and John and my baby, and this earth. So many unknowns. And the wallpaper intuits my doubt, feeds off my straying, flutters, waits and watches. Readies for battle.

10

Jennie, 2020

Re: First Miracle Continued . . .

DEAR BISHOP MONROE,

I write with an aching hand and my eyes failing me. I will continue straightaway with discussion related to what occurred after the first miracle, so as not to waste time. Maribel requests that I take it easy, doctor's orders. She claims the writing is consuming too much of my energy. Maribel does not understand the magnitude of my undertaking.

It was in the hospital that Jane confided in me, explained the time of the séance, when she heard a voice and knew it was a man of God. The voice told her to go to the creek. He promised to save her so she would save others. It was a test of faith, she'd said. I didn't believe her at the time and worried for her. My poor Jane is suicidal, delusional, I'd thought. But I wouldn't' dare tell anyone for fear they'd commit her, and I'd never see her again, or they'd do horrific things to her, restrain her, medicate her, change her. Treatment of the mentally ill has become more humane today. Back in the 40's I'm afraid, it was inhumane. So I was fearful. I was selfish that way, Your Reverence, I worried for her, wanted my Jane to be the same one I always knew. I'd felt abandoned, felt like I lost

41

my sister, my best friend, my own soul, even if she was chosen. And I'll confess, Your Reverence, a part of me was mad at a God who would take her away from me. Another part of me remained uncertain. Maybe she needed doctors. Maybe I was wrong. Maybe my dearest Jane needed help I couldn't give her. And I even considered she might be dangerous. I became wary around her. It became unsettling. I examined her gestures, her words, her silence. I was on high alert. What I didn't know at the time was how I, too, was being tested. My loyalty to Jane, to her faith would, eventually, fortify my faith as well. At the time, being ten-years old, I wasn't sure what to believe. But then I had to consider, if it wasn't God, or some divine being, then it had to be of an evil origin. How would I discern? Or what if she leapt into the creek on purpose, to end her life? What would be the next command? All of these concerns haunted me day in and out and for the rest of the summer, until the next miracle occurred. After the second occurrence, I couldn't deny it but questioned my own sanity. It became more complicated, rather than less, and I suffered. I will end here, Your Reverence, as I need to take my rest.

    Yours in Christ,
    Jennie Wright

Re: Transformation

Your Reverence,

    Not to belabor the point, but I feel more is required regarding her deterioration and how Jane altered in ways after the incident in the creek. She was so young when it occurred and seemed to age way beyond her years. I waited for something cataclysmic to happen. But everything returned to normalcy, the way it does at the end of the summer. One difference was that Jane had to leave a month earlier. We all hugged her, teary-eyed, especially since we'd almost lost her, and Eda got her off on the train. She returned to her house in Concord and sent me pictures of her first day in sixth grade. She rarely went to school that year, as she refused to read the secular writing, as she referred to the curriculum. The following summer, after the second miracle, where she brought Melissa Haighworth back to life, and it hit the news, she was bullied and stopped going altogether. Eda obtained tutors for her.

I looked forward to the holidays when I knew I'd see her again, but some part of me felt disconnected from her. In her letters, Jane seemed changed. She wrote how much she missed me, and how the event changed her, and she wasn't sure exactly how. I recall asking her, before she left, if she really believed it was God. "Of course," she'd said, and her eyes lit up in some kind of hazy, delirious manner. After each of her letters, she'd include scripture.

She came for thanksgiving with her mother, Ruth. John nudged me when Jane stepped off the train. Jane was wearing a long skirt with tights, and her hair was braided and pulled back in a high bun. She seemed older than her years, priggish, more like a librarian or a schoolmarm. And most glaring of all was the Bible she was clutching under her arm. Forgive me, Father, but, admittedly, I had to stifle an impulse to laugh. John, too. We were both of that age, teetering on the brink of adulthood but still childish in many ways. It was John who shushed me. Being two years older, he had the good sense to behave, and, as I said, he had a special fondness for Jane. We both did, but his was becoming something more. I asked her later, as we were settling her in, how she liked the Bible, as I noted how she kissed it before putting it atop her bureau, and she told me it was the best book she'd ever read. She said I need to read it. When I asked why, she'd turned to me, a deadpan expression, and said, "For your salvation." And it gave me the chills, admittedly.

So I tried, Your Reverence, but I bored of it quickly, finding it too difficult to comprehend. Jane carried it with her everywhere. And we'd eventually learned to accept our new Jane—Bible, and all.

At any rate, it was part of her transformation, and my reaction to it. The initial confused state of mind, the paranoia, and then the acceptance.

The sun is so bright today, Your Reverence, I can barely see the page. I've been having trouble with my eyes as of late, and the glaucoma is worsening. I worry that soon I will lose my sight. It's only a matter of time, I'm afraid. By God's grace, I'm still able to see that this point. I can't imagine not completing my letter to you. It's imperative that we move on now, to the second miracle. It wasn't until she turned twelve, two years later, when the second occurrence happened. I call it the second miracle, when Jane healed Eda. I will have to continue tomorrow as my eyes require rest.

Your loyal servant in Christ,
Jennie Wright

11

Jane, 1950

September 23

ANY DAY NOW. ANY day. I can barely write. I'm trembling, Jennie.
I woke to the fluttering, the yellow strips flapping, wildly, in some
invisible vile draft. I try to think of better days, a time when I felt
safe, a time when we hunted for sea glass and scaled the jetty and
tunneled beneath the cottage. I miss those times, the dampened
sand, the cool feel of it. Now the tunnel is long since been filled in.
And back then, too, the window opened, and the salt air soothed
all that ailed. Now the window is nailed shut due to some long-
standing issue with critters burrowing into the walls and gnawing
wires. It's not for you, Jennie. Not now. Our hideaway is changed,
and not for the better. The air is thick and dank and the cobwebs
sway in the rafters. I imagine spiders dropping down onto my bed
with their venom and eggs. The wallpaper we liked to pick at is still
here, and it's dingier, peeling more aggressively, hanging in horrid
strips like an abomination. And even the sun, our beloved sun,
the sun we welcomed, now bothers. When it finds its way into the
attic, it's sharp and blinding, at times. Or it's divine but ungraspable. I recall a time we craved the sun, floating in the Sound on the
maroon raft, kicking and paddling with youthful strength fueled

by adrenaline, our fresh, rich blood, our bodies drying beneath the blaze like two basilisks, and I pine for it. I pine for a sun I once knew, to be stretched across the raft, the two of us. And I can't help but think of my soul, my sister, sailing the seas with Maxwell, and I wonder. . .Will I ever see my Jennie again?

Later . . .

The pains are closer together, Jennie. I'm so alone. I need you! I'll be a mother and you're not here for me. Is this my new divine purpose? I can't help myself. I return to the past, to the time I changed. No one believed me, then, of course, not even you, my sister, my soul, not even you, Jennie, and I was returned home to those doctors who poked and prodded my body and mind. I was referred to as deluded, psychotic. I'd wanted to write to you, to confide in you about the visions, the words, the incarnation, the miracle of my own resurrection. But even you, even my dearest friend, my confidante, I could never trust. I knew the outcome, even before it happened, the hospital stays, the evaluations, the persecution. I knew the prophesy, the divine plan. I was to suffer for their infirmities, manifest Jesus' wounds. I accepted it.

The pain is persistent. And I go back to that time. Clearing my mind is not a possibility, as with each pain it returns more viscerally.

September 24

I explained to Maribel how the attic makes me anxious. Maribel reassured me, said it was the nesting period. Then she sat in the wicker chair, which is unusual, and she stared off in the distance. After a brief pause, she recollected her own experience, preparing for her baby. She described the fear and excitement. "But then something happened," she'd said, and her eyes watered, and she struggled to continue. "My baby girl was stillborn. She came out blue," she blurted out, as if it were an afterthought, and her voice turned lower, and eerie. She gave me a chill. I was dumbstruck, paralyzed, said how awful it must have been. She came over to me then, regained her composure. I took her hand and it jarred her back, and she explained, in a lighter, more pragmatic tone, how she'd been sick throughout the pregnancy and knew something was off. "You're fine. Don't you worry, Janie." She squeezed my arm. She hadn't used the name, Janie, since I was small. I think it's got to her, the dark presence beneath the wallpaper.

Later . . .

I had a horrible nightmare. My baby came out blue. I woke gasping for air, delirious. Please, God. Save her! I prayed and prayed! And then John popped in and said, "Almost time," and I could have hit him! I've decided if he says it again, I'll tell him to stop saying it, confess that it only serves to agitate and make things worse, make me less apt to sleep, make me think of something cataclysmic. It's our pain to bear. *Unto the woman I will greatly multiply thy sorrow and thy conception. . .*It worsens with the thought of scripture. I try to stand, to retrieve Bonaventure, the Seraphic Doctor, seeking philosophy, wisdom, but it's agonizing to move, so I'm forced to stay in bed. I can no longer continue this.

Update . . .

The sun is up now and it's checkering the floor. Soon the knocking. Soon. And I'll have to say come in, and he'll be aghast when he sees me. I tried to get up. I tried, I'll explain. But the pain is worse and his words, It's almost time, just the idea of it makes me queasy, light-headed. *Lord, take this cup, not by my will but thine.* And shouldn't I accept this as Godly, ordained? How does it happen that a small, helpless baby can inflict so much pain? The sin of Eve. The pain we must bear.

September 25

Still it's in me. I can't eat, Jennie. Maribel scares me. I'm sorry for her, and for her loss, but she scares me now that I know what happened to her. I wish she hadn't told me. I feel as if she's contagious, somehow, cursed. I know that's an awful thought to have and wrong and sinful, because she is so helpful to me and always has been. I should be charitable. I should love her as I love you. I should love everyone as my sister and brother.

"Soon. . .very soon now, Jane," he says, and this time Maribel nods her head, solemn in her eyes and mouth. Even she, like the wallpaper, has a new darkness inside. She hides her hair behind a scarf. Her wrinkled eyes are glazed. And it makes me all the more despondent. Maribel's solemn look, and her gaze, unsettles me. She's changed. I'm sure of it. Such strange solemnity, as if from a secret, something unholy and dark when these times should be revered and joyous. And if you were here with me, Jennie, then it would be just that, joyous, a time of elation, celebration. But she's all I have, Maribel, and she nods, reticently, and there it is again and again, that deep solemnity, rearing its ugly head, and I'm convinced, yes, that it contributes to my nightmares and paralysis, my state of mind and moods, my wakeful nights and insomnia.

Update . . .

I'm crippled by pain. Maribel brings me more of the pills. I don't mind her scarf so much now. And I can sleep, dreamless.

The pains are closer together . . . a sharp one throttles me, brings on an array, a kaleidoscope of reds and violets and yellows, all shades. I hear, Maribel say, Jane, it's time.

Breathe.

12

Jennie, 2020

Re: The Second Miracle

Dear Bishop Monroe,

Prior to the second miracle, we were preparing for the yearly scavenger hunt, reviewing the list of items: purple sand, one conch shell, one black bow tie, one grey striped necktie, two crabs, three muscles. I'm amazed at my memories for such sundry items. It was one of our most cherished times. Jane was energetic, and I tried to be enthusiastic, but our mother, Eda, and her illness, overshadowed the event. John promised he'd sit with her, and it would be the first hunt he'd miss. We never worried about Eda. Our mother was always healthy, always there for us, taking care of us when we were scared or ill. Now, she could barely walk or eat. She had taken ill a few days prior and was bedridden. John mentioned a doctor, but Eda refused, said it was the flu and that she'd shake it off. But she grew weaker each day, weaker than we'd ever found her to be. On the fourth evening, John said she hadn't touched her dinner, and she was wheezing. I insisted we call the doctor, but Eda sat up and ate her soup, insisting she was fine. Her temperature was down, and she was chatting and livelier than she'd been in days, inquiring about the scavenger hunt, apologizing for missing it as she usually liked to help out. John was still asleep. All seemed well. I even felt her forehead and she was cooler to the touch. With what seemed like good news, we went to bed feeling lighter, less concerned.

The following morning, I woke earlier than usual from a disturbing dream, and hurried to Eda's bedroom. I noticed the smell first—a metallic sweetness. And I felt an unnatural stillness. I rushed over to her bedside and shook her, panic-stricken. Your Reverence, I can't articulate in writing the fear I felt at the time, the idea of losing Eda, my dear mother. It's a strange propensity we have to take a thing for granted. I could barely breathe. At some point, Jane entered the room. I must have been screeching and not aware of it. Jane stretched herself out on top of Eda, and began caressing her cheek and forehead. Her mouth was moving in prayer. It wasn't time for strange behavior, I'd considered. Eda was close to death. "We need to call an ambulance," I finally uttered, although I've no idea how it exited my mouth. At this point, Your Reverence, I was on the ground. I couldn't stand and I was suffering from some sort of a partial shock. I was on my knees, my head lowered, unable to look at the scene, to observe my poor mother motionless. One can't predict one's frame of mind at the time of trauma. I became child-like, Your Reverence, closed my eyes tight, as if I might make it all go away. If I didn't see it, then it didn't exist. In the back of my mind, I knew what was true. Mother was dead. My dear, Eda was gone. Father was gone. And now she was gone, too. No amount of praying or comforting touches could bring her back. Still, Jane was indifferent, defiant, kept on with the murmuring, and it was like needles pricking my skin. We need to call an ambulance, I was thinking, but I couldn't move a muscle, and the words were trapped inside of me. I can't tell you how much time went by before John came bursting into the room, and I heard him shout, "Mother! What Happened? Are you okay?" I couldn't have known that he was speaking to our mother who was now sitting upright by some miraculous intervention, unbeknownst to me, as I was crouched down low to the ground, with my hands over my face. Yes, Your Reverence, our dear mother, Eda, was alive and well. All color had returned to her cheeks. She was breathing.

She was holding Jane's hand in both of hers and thanking her, repeatedly, "Lord, thank you." I was baffled. I was dumbfounded, stymied. Just a few minutes ago, Eda was lifeless, pale, cold, and there was no pulse, no pulse. . .just like Jane. But somehow, she was alive, resurrected. . .just like Jane. I was in denial, and maybe shock, and I didn't want to believe Jane had anything to do with it. But then the way she looked at Jane, and the way Eda held onto her hands, gripped her. There was something intangible, an undeniable presence.

And that's when it took hold of me, Your Reverence. I was her closet ally. We were closer than any two living creatures can be, Jane and I, like one mind, one organism. But what Jane did to Eda seemed to sever us. We were no longer equals. I felt cast off, excised from her. I couldn't deny the look in my mother's eyes, or Jane's. Whatever Jane did to Eda, whatever powers she summoned, healed our mother of all sickness, brought her back from the dead. I, the other hand, did nothing. I was useless to my own mother, I'd decided. It was a defining moment. Jane and I were no longer one. She'd performed the impossible, a miracle. How many times had I heard Jane say, With God all things are possible. I couldn't accept it. Why, Jane? Eda had been beyond reviving. She was dead to me, and I could do nothing to bring her back. So I'd gotten down low, as low to the ground as I could get. If I could have burrowed beneath the floorboards, I would have done it. I would have died with her, Your Excellency. I would have died with my dear mother. I know it's wrong, and to end one's life is a mortal sin, but none of that mattered. I couldn't live without Eda. I didn't deserve to live. I should die with her. Why should I still be alive and breathing? I'd thought to myself.

But then she was revived, somehow, and something in me snapped. I should have been relieved. I should have hugged her, but, instead, I kept my distance, observed the two holding each other in thankful praise, and I was invisible. I was left to ponder my futility. I was no more useful than the ant that scurried past me. I couldn't talk or move. I stayed there on the floor. It became about me, and only me. I was full of pity, self-absorbed and sinful, detestable, filled with an envious rage. She did this. Jane. She had some divine power bestowed on her. It was Jane who was chosen to save Eda. Why her? I couldn't do anything for Eda. I was cast off, dispensable.

"She was dead," I said then. And they looked down at me, all three of them, John and Jane and Eda between them on the bed. I stood up this time. "She was dead."

No one said a word. They glared back at me. I know now they were waiting with extraordinary patience and humility for me to come to my senses, to overcome my shock, to join them.

And so I did. I reached out and touched Jane on the shoulder and my hand shook. "It was you," I said to her.

"Not by my will," she returned.

I know now, although I have no evidence Eda had stopped breathing, I know it to be true. And I know now, just like the disciples were endowed with the Holy Ghost's power of healing and resurrecting, so, too, was Jane on that July morning when she resurrected my mother, Eda.

Until tomorrow.

Yours faithfully in Christ,

Jennie Wright

13

Jane, 1950

September 26

I SLEPT ON THE floor, Jennie. The wallpaper was flapping like a fledgling baby bird fallen from the nest. I got out of bed this time, moved in closer, and to my disgust, saw it was teeming with centipedes and oversized beetles creeping out of every crevice. I lunged at it and scraped and clawed at it, and the bugs took refuge on my skin, crawled on my hands and up my arms and in my hair. I swatted and thrashed and lost my balance and fell backwards onto the ground. I stayed there for a time, and I found a long-forgotten peace, recalled Bonaventure, considered the variety of things, the multitude, the beauty and the light and the fixtures, all things made for us, the power of things. And I thought of you, Jennie, After warming ourselves by the fire chilly June mornings, when the morning fog lifted, when the seagulls screeched overhead, when our maroon raft bobbed up and down over the waves, and we watched the light play off all forms—the jetty, the cottages, the shore, the hairs on our heads, our arms. You'd get out before me, shivering and hungry. I'd go alone, drift off into the silence, found my nourishment, past the dock, past the jetty, to vast places beyond the smallness, and you'd stayed back on the shore, fading faster, mouth open in a howl, arms gyrating, frantically, as if to lose me would be to lose your soul.

Update . . .

The pain returns, sharp and relentless, and I'm breathless. I was in and out. I heard them on the stairs like a thundering herd.

September 27

It's done. An oddness pervades. Mirabal leaves food on trays and sneers. The silence is palpable. My refuge turned on me. My eyes rest on the wallpaper. It peels and flakes and mocks and swirls, pointed and sharp like fangs. I'm easier prey now. The sacred is out of me. It could eat me if it wanted. It could take me into its folds, ravage me. I'm numb but for the paper, mesmerizing, bewitching. I've taken to staring at it for inordinate amounts of time. God's wrath is upon me. I'm in purgatory awaiting judgement. Judge me lightly, Oh, Lord! Pray for me, Jennie! Who else? Am I dead, Jennie? Women die from childbirth. But then how could it be that I'm still here in such a physical state, reeling from aches and pains? Maybe I'm in the other place, where the damned go. And maybe the pain will increase, and all light will cease to be, and my flesh will blister and ooze and heal and then blister all over again. Am I the chaff which the wind drives away? Will I perish? Oh, Jennie! Pray for me, Jennie!

Update . . .

Something is awry. John came to me. He stood over me holding a bundle in his arms. "Our baby girl, Jane. Look what you did, Jane. Look what you did," he said, holding it out to me. He wanted me to take it, to take the blame. I covered my eyes. I couldn't look. I shook, uncontrollably, Jennie. I'm all about me. I imagine vain things, only myself. What will happen to me? I'm vexed!

What did I do? What? I tried to ask, but my voice quivered. He stared back puzzled, and then I heard screams from him, or me, or somewhere, and they were like the anguished suffering of one tormented, and from an unthinkable region, one in which I'd never been, one in which I'm sure, in short time, I'll be sent to. What did I do? I wanted to say. What did I do? He stepped back towards the door, clutching the bundle, horror painted on his face, and I imagined how I must appear to him, disfigured, maligned, revolting, and I shrunk further into myself and for something I can't fathom. It is not for me to know what God has in store for me.

He left me, and now it's the final wrung, and I feel it taking hold, a shiver like the onset of a fever, a chill at the base of my neck working its way down. And the paper mocks me. The lines twist and turn and grimace, soon it will lash out at me, dash me into pieces. Blessed are the ones who trust in God. Jennie, come to me. Tell me I'm worthy!

It will never be as it once was before the deed, whatever it was I did.

Update!

Good news! All my angst was for naught! God is merciful! He gave me a healthy baby girl! I'm forgiven! God's mercy endures forever! Helen is alive and perfectly healthy! How could I have entertained the other? What made me entertain the malefice? John blames the pills and hormone fluctuations. I blame the tempter, the wallpaper, the apostate angel's guile.

Even so, it was bliss. God is generous in his gifts! I fed her for the first time. She clung to me, pulled from me a source of milky life. God is a shield for me. . . and for Helen!

But John remains puzzled. He sat across from us in the wicker chair. He worries. I imagine it's some involuntary countenance, a melancholy or fear affixed to my face, a residual anxiety.

"I'll be back," he said. "Maribel will sit with you."

I apologized.

"No, stop, darling," he said, and "It's not your fault. I love you. You know that, right?"

Yes. Of course, I told him. I love you too! And I do, Jennie. I do love him.

He kissed my cheek and moved my hair away from my face, so gently, and it thrilled me. My flesh tingles but not from him alone, no, but from another source, one new to me, an untainted soul resting on my breast. My lovely Helen.

Motherhood is pure bliss.

September 28

Bliss is fleeting, Jennie. The wallpaper has ruined me. I cried onto the Lord and he heard me and now it's returned. I should not be afraid. I'm armed. But the rustling started and I was drawn away from Helen, lured to it. Helen became distraught and pulled away. I hugged her tightly to me. At that point, John was at my side, prying my flesh and bones, my soul, my sweet, sweet angel, out of my arms, telling me I needed to rest, and she's had enough to eat, and anything he could say to get her away from me.

Update . . .

I was so relieved, Jennie. He brought her to me. But my relief was short-lived. I tried, Jennie. I tried to keep my eyes fixed on her, despite the dark presence, the pricking presence of the wallpaper. It watches me and waits for me to notice. If I'm brave enough, I glance over at it, but only when Helen is not with me. I try to see beneath and the closer I inspect, the more I'm convinced it's an anomaly, cleverly orchestrated. The lines move and twist, as if they are tangling in upon themselves, purposefully, to confuse me. Each day it changes, makes itself indecipherable, tricks, confounds. I've considered there's a catalyst, some force within it, compelling it, feeding it.

I'm all aware of dark forces, the way it latches on, feeds on souls, like the bullies who attacked me after school, set their hearts against me, against God, emulating a corrupt and crooked people. I see their faces, now, in my mind's eye, distorted and vile, behind the brick wall, waiting to grab me and drag me down. One pulled out scissors, and I feared he'd stab me. They sat on me, spit on me, called me a witch, cut off chunks of my hair, punched me until my nose bled. It was the last time I went to a public school, Jennie. Did I ever tell you? My mother reported it. I begged her not to, said I forgave them. The bad was cast out, like the apostate angels, who devised evil plots, thrived on other's pain and torments. The Lord abhors the deceitful. The bullies were expelled. God is merciful.

Now the vile creatures return to me, seethe and salivate, seeking retribution.

They'll have no way with me. I'm armed with God's divine wisdom. I tacked a sheet up over the wallpaper.

September 29

Maribel brought her to me, crying. She latched on quickly and drifted off to sleep. But too soon she woke. Her countenance tugged at my heart. Her wide-eyes unhinged me. Her cries pierced my soul. Maribel rushed in and pried her out of my arms, insisting she take my sweet, Helen, as if I meant her harm. I'm overcome, distraught! I pray for reason, to dismiss all fleeting thoughts and imaginings. Oh, if I could think like John, be John. Free my mind of these ill thoughts, quell my anxieties, dismiss the false with a wave of my hand. But what of the unseen? But then I'd let my guard down. And who will deny the subtle ways of the apostate angels, the militant, relentless, immortal, thriving on pain and suffering. Maybe when we were young and unsuspecting, Jennie, when our souls were unmarred, it crept beneath the walls, waiting for this moment. Maybe that's why I'm back here to suffer for it.

What, Jennie, what will I tell her? My God, my conduit, will he speak for me? In the way Aaron spoke for Moses, will someone speak for me? Will you? Will John? But if it's me, I pray God arms me with the right words, cleanses my words, gives me the strength to say what I need to say to her. How do I prepare her if she's chosen, too? What if an angel of God speaks to her? How will she receive it? Is it genetic these matters? Why was I chosen? Why was I considered up to the task, Jennie, and how does it come to others? What if Helen were to reject her inner voice, turn against it, and lose her sense of goodness, her sense of the truth, her grip on reality? My inner soul spoke to me, and I submitted. I had no idea what was in store for me. The visions of glory and pain and suffering overtook me. When I fell into the icy cold waters, I ascended and emerged, washed. When I was pulled ashore, I remembered it clearly. An angel of God spoke to me, told me I had a mission to heal and to save others, to unite believers in one body of Christ. So few believed me. I kept things in my heart. How will I make her believe? Nothing is accomplished but by God's will. I am weak, Jennie, trembling. Be a shield for me! Save me, Oh my God!

Now the sounds of my sweet Helen in the stairwell!

September 30

I pray these words pierce your soul! I imagine her hungry cries, but I'm mistaken. I heard the creaks on the stair, and it was Maribel with my breakfast. I inquired about her, and Maribel stared back, strangely. "She's being fed. You need your rest this morning, dear." And then she was silent, and I was tongue-tied, spent of all courage, an empty vessel. I wanted to scream, demand she bring my baby to me. Perhaps I'm slipping down into the abyss, to St. John's dark night, where light is hidden, where the soul is purged of all senses and pleasures, where I'll lose all hope and all track of time, so that it will seem, for me, an eternal despair, where the soul is emptied. If so, what if I should emerge from it. Only the worthiest return.

Again, I hear her small whimpering in the stairwell. I pray it's real this time.

Update . . .

Once again, my hopes are crushed. Oh, Jennie, some darkness tricks my mind, and I hear my sweet Helen's cries day and night like an endless lamenting. The room is dim and the sheet has fallen. I opened the door a crack and called out to her. Nothing but the dark night. Destroy the ill doers, Oh God! I pray and pray. I tried to reattach the wallpaper but felt faint. The wallpaper blows, erratically, insultingly, as if it intuits my desire for purity. I feel as if it's increased in size. A vile entity hides beneath it and I think of my assaulter. He took me and pinned me down, called me Jezebel. This one wanted something from me. He ripped my shirt. He wanted to do worse with me. And he would have but for the grace of God. A tall and stately stranger appeared, an angel in the form of man, interceded, and his very presence sent the boy fleeing. "Forgive your enemies," the stranger said to me, before a cloud took him up. He was not of this earth, but a messenger of God. Now the paper flutters and whips about and mocks me, because it knows I know the nature of it, the measure of evil lurking in secret places. No hiding for the wicked. I've encountered it before, many times, manifested in those who turn away from God's graces. I know much is asked of me, and I need to forgive, lose all bitterness, all spite, and quell my fears. I'm God's creation, made in his own image. I need to remember, lest I forget my origins and stew in malice, become easy prey for my offenders.

The resistance will be fierce. I should be armed with the shield of prayer and faith. I should be steady on my feet, unbending in my faith. But how will I do it, Jennie? I'm weak, emptied, left with a residue of verses and faint inclinations. I'm all carnality, tethered to my aches and pains and emotions. The tiniest flutter of the paper sends me reeling. Arm me, Oh, God! Be my shield!

When will I see her, oh my sweet, sweet Helen?

October 1

Where are my tidings of joy? Where is my jubilation? I'm tethered to her, to my flesh and blood. Like the workers of iniquity, I'm tormented. My soul is out of reach. Images haunt me, those of her cherubic face twisted in turmoil, crying out for me. I can barely imagine it, the ache is too much to bear. I want to hold her and soothe her. Temptations ensure, and I glance over at the wallpaper's dinginess, the despair of it, the decadence, and consider it's unhealthy for her soul. Our last feeding it caught my eye and then held me there, fixed to it. I'd lost a will power to look away, as if a dark entity fixed me to it. The peeling scraped my soul. The swerving lines, like venomous tendrils, mesmerized, to the point that when I returned to Helen, she was distraught, red-faced, milk seeping out over her small, blistered lips. Oh, Jennie, if you were here with me, I'd be stronger. You'd support me. I'm her mother.

Babies need their mothers for comfort. Be my anchor! Oh, God deliver my soul!

I'm alone, Jennie, and you are too far away from me, and it makes me profoundly sad, if I should consider it too much.

And then I consider vanity, my desire to be saved, my selfish need for mercy, my delving into self-pity. It is by his will. And if I am to suffer, thy will be done. How must our Immaculate Mary have felt when she witnessed her beloved son tortured, falling in the dirt, or being nailed to the cross, suffering such agony for us. I must be patient, submit to my circumstances. John says it's for the best. I should trust in God's plan. I told you, Jennie, I sense his presence. He comes to me. But I can't admit it. No. John will decide I'm unstable, or delusional. I pray silently, and out of his view. If he or Maribel were to catch me, they might keep her from me. The stakes are too high this time. They'll hospitalize me, return me to the sisters, to Mother of Mercy Home, and I may never see my darling Helen again. As much as I love the sisters, I love my attachments. I love my Helen more. I love my family, my husband and my life, and the cottage. The material consumes me. Does that mean I'm rejecting God's demands? Am I a defector? Have I chosen the darker path of earthly desires? No, it can't be. Motherhood is sacred. If I should leave here, go outside and walk the jetty, stand at the edge of the water, let the spray of the ocean anoint me, I'd be healed.

I pray you are thinking of me, Jennie. I like to think there on the glimmering seas, your mind drifts off to me. I pray for you every day. I try to remember that with God all things are possible.

I was saved for this. I wish I could tell you. But you've gone to sea with Maxwell. I'm selfish. I want you here. And I can't help but wonder why you left. Was it because of me? Did you fear me? Did you need to get away from me? I pray you forgive me. I disappointed you. I changed. I had no choice but to go to the creek. God commissioned me. I was chosen. Why me, Jennie? I can't say. God's mysterious ways evade me.

And then I consider, maybe it was never true, none of it, and it fills me with inexplicable dread. I have no one to affirm it was not a dream or a hallucination—the creek, all of it. If I truly had a psychosis, then I wouldn't know what was true. My hallucinations would be my reality. I can't help but entertain the idea. It explains my true nature, why I'm despairing. I've tried to repress it, my desire to contemplate it, the creature behind the wall. What if no amount of praying will absolve me? I'm guilty of vanity, of unguarded thoughts, drawn to the darkness, a crime too heinous to admit. It's not the wallpaper. No, it's much more. The wallpaper is merely a receptacle for the corruption. And I seek it out with a sort of lustful wanting, an insatiable thirst, fix my eyes on it, on the meandering lines, twisting and turning in upon themselves, an eternal damnation, festering, the decadence of ancient scents, the layers of history and decay and meaning in there, beyond my scope, beyond what even sentient sinners can imagine. And still, with an acute awareness, I ache to touch it, run my hands along it, trace the lines, be taken into its folds, to a soulless journey.

Now there are the wails beyond, the screeches, high pitched and steely. God incline thine ear. I can't reach her. I'm here and she's far, a figment of my imagination, ungraspable to even my mind's eye. All good is beyond me. Lead me, Oh, Lord, to the righteous way! I'm as a vapor, a breath of wind seeking refuge! All for Helen, so she can know the way to God. Give me words to confess to her how I was taunted and despised, deemed deluded, a threat to society. I will risk so much in the telling. Who will she believe. . ..me or them? We are born flawed, prey for the apostates, vulnerable to the false gods. Not one of us is more perfect than the other. All will be judged by the one supreme God, our immortal creator. A pure heart is filled with mercy. She'll demand to see some evidence. What do I give her beyond my words? Will my words be enough?

I pray she'll forgive me, and she'll come to know the path of righteousness, if I tell her these things, plainly and simply, in way she can know it. I can't fathom the notion of my sweet Helen rejecting me. Yet I doubt myself. True believers never doubt their own salvation. What does that make me but a hypocrite.

You see, Jennie, how much I need you! Oh, Jennie, I pray these words reach you, beyond the page, across the seas, and draw you back to me. I'm conflicted and I realize I can't do this alone. Helen needs her Aunt Jennie. I need my sister, my soul.

October 2

The air is cooler. It has me in its icy grip. I fed her today. I kept her bundled up. I kept my eyes on her at all times. I felt her goodness course through my veins, despite the dark presence. I pray for deliverance, remembering some verses. I improvised. God knows my intent. Still, I'm weakened by the malevolence. And it's becoming more difficult to perceive, to understand my situation. The presence is menacing, lurking beneath, submerged like sludge and mire, salivating for my soul. I have never been surer of a thing. It is an immeasurable force, Jennie, inside the wallpaper. It watches me and waits for me to notice. It thrives on my pain. It's more alive than ever. If I'm brave enough, I glance over at it, but only when Helen is not with me. I try to see it, to study it. Some part of me that feeds it thinks I can conquer it alone, with my will. The lines move and twist and confound—hypnotic, bewitching. The apostate is clever, full of trickery and guile. Just when I think I've figured out, the code changes and it alters. One subtle change is enough to conceal its core.

You disliked it more than me, Jennie. I wanted so much to loathe it. Back then it was innocuous, merely an eye sore. You called it horrid. We laughed at the word, horrid. You suggested we rip it off. You picked at it, peeled it. Maybe we fed it, somehow, our disgust with it. I'd considered there's some force within it, feeding it, a harbinger of evil tidings. If I admitted to this, I risk never seeing my sweet Helen again. How then would I guide her, protect her from the evil?

Are those footsteps I hear?

I pray my words are reaching you in spirit, Jennie!

Update . . .

Jennie, I used a bit of ingenuity and am taking every precaution. I ensure the sheet is tacked up over the wallpaper. When Helen is brought to me for feedings, I keep my precious darling hidden beneath the blankets, lightly enough so she can breathe, of course. I need to protect her from the creature. She's easy prey and so small and helpless. She nurses, voraciously, as if she portends a dark invasion, and her final meal. She barely whimpers. If she does, I hum to her and she calms. When I do, the wallpaper settles. Now I pray for her, prayers of deliverance and protection. Verses return to me, slowly. I can't recall them all verbatim. God knows my intent. I have to believe it. I wish so much I had my rosary and prayer books. But John won't allow it. He'd call the doctors. You know Jennie, how important it is for me to stay as far away as possible from the doctors and their drugs. I try so hard to recall the prayers, the words. Each day some of it returns to me. God knows what's in my heart. My true intent is what God measures. Still, I think of the hermits in the caves praying hundreds of psalms by memory, and I feel inadequate. Why can't I remember God's words? How did I fall away so easily? Was it the consummation of my marriage? Did it turn me towards lust and earthly things? I should have stayed with the sisters, Jennie, lived a life of solitude and prayer. It was my purpose. But John loved me too much, and he lured me away, convinced me we were soulmates. Should I be punished for loving my soul? I loved him, too. I do love him with all my heart. But maybe in the sharing of love the bond is diminished, rather than fortified. The once untarnished love becomes parceled and, therefore, less. Tell me, Jennie! I need your words!

October 3

Now if Helen is not with me, I gasp for air. Words return to me . . . *for there is no faithfulness . . . inward parts are wickedness . . . they flatter with their tongues.* How will I protect her now and in the future? She'll be accosted by doubters, those who decry the gospel, who refer to it as frivolous, claim Jesus was not the Messiah, that Jesus was not resurrected, that it's scientifically impossible. They'll preach to her with fancy tongue and eloquence, tell her it's a myth, try to convince her Jesus was fabricated, embellished, to quell the agony of our mortality. Even as I write this, my hand trembles.

63

I fear for myself, for my own salvation. To know it so well is to have reflected on it, experienced it. Are these my beliefs? Once I believed, wholly. I knew in my heart, Jesus Christ was more than a man, that he was God's son, the incarnated word, born to save us from ourselves, from our sins, to redeem us. I wanted to be him, to live like him, to suffer for other's sins. Jesus was rejected, too, displaced in society, believed to be born out of wedlock. Visiting the temple he found his roots, his place, his purpose. Most never do find their purpose. Will Helen find hers, amidst the tumult and backlash? I need to warn her of the temptations, our weakness, how the tangible is easier to accept, how it might seem implausible, outrageous even to accept God is incarnated in Jesus Christ and Jesus was both human and God. I have to believe, Jennie, eventually, she'll find her way, and her eyes will open to a new truth, one that is untainted by the material world. But she'll have to arm herself, expect to be rejected, scorned, shunned by many, even adults and those closest to her. As I write this, the wallpaper scrapes and flutters, as if to halt my words.

Never!

You shunned me, Jennie. You sailed far away from me. You believed I was deluded, unstable. I made you uncomfortable. Fear took over. We are fallible, Jennie, all of us. I forgive you!

Are those footsteps I hear?

I've only looked at the sheet once this morning. I keep my eyes peeled to the window. The sun beams in now like assurance from above, the Holy Spirit in the spiraling particles.

I pray for Helen. I pray for you, too, Jennie. I pray you return to me. I pray for your soul. I worry the waves will engulf you and you'll die without grace. I worry for your salvation. Is your name in the book of life? Is mine? Is John's? Are you forgiven? I pray for you. And John too. I pray hardest for him. I can pray for other's salvation. I'll tell her that, too, that she should always pray for the sinners, always. God is merciful.

October 4

John brought Helen to me this morning and her eyes were puffy. My worst fear is that she's being left to cry it out. I would never espouse to that cruel method of training. Or the notion that it's good for her lungs. Crying is an infant's voice, expressing some discomfort or loneliness, and it's imperative she is tended to immediately. You'd agree with me, Jennie! I know you would! But when I explained all this to Maribel, she said nothing, but merely nodded her head in agreement, as if she were simply placating me. Her eyes were blank with indifference. And Helen was flushed and warmer than usual. I've decided to discuss it with John. You'd agree with me, Jennie. We have the same heart. Maribel has her own manner of doing things and she has never had a child herself, although she lost a child. Not that it should matter in a worthy soul. Some of the holiest choose to marry Christ and devote their lives to their devotions. It's an unusual sacrifice, not an easy one for the nurturing soul to make. Even Faustina doubted her profession, experienced a darkness in her soul during her novitiate, or as she put it, when she had "a shadow over her soul" the closer she was to her vows. Perhaps it was the nurturing part of her that imagined marriage and motherhood. Yet it would seem she had no choice. Each time she tried to abandon her faith, Jesus interceded, or even the Blessed Mary, and she returned back on course and remained steadfast. In her diary, she expresses that "strangeness" and "darkness" where she could barely meditate or pray or decipher what she read. The words no longer seemed to touch her heart. When she expressed her troubles she was told these were her trials and she'd have to suffer through while remaining obedient to God's guidance. She was troubled by those who suggested she was deluded and not saintly enough to have Jesus come to her and speak to her. I can't help but cry when I read of her troubles, comparing my own to hers in ways, feeling a similar sense of abandonment and confusion. Faustina came to realize the confessor was not always receptive. A sensitive soul can easily be misunderstood and dismissed. Faustina wavered at these times, when she was young and teetering on the brink of womanhood and needing affirmation by her trusted confessors, but also wanting to remain obedient to her inner voice, which she knew to be Jesus.

God's voice has been missing for some time. I wonder if my inner voice, my compassion, is the voice of God. My desire for Helen conflicts me further. I miss her terribly. I wake frequently to what sounds like Helen's cries. At one point I thought it was coming from behind the wall. I got out of bed and went to the wallpaper. I was close enough to smell the mold and decadence emanating from it, saw what seemed to be eyes peering out from beneath the pattern, searing my soul. Meanwhile, the cries continued deep within the walls, and my heart raced. I wanted to tear at it, destroy it to get to her. But something stopped me. My inner voice, perhaps, told me to return to bed. Had I given into the temptation, who knows what might have happened. Delusional thoughts trick me. God guides me, as he did with Faustina. I can't permit the dark tempters to invade my soul. I must remain convicted to my purpose. Do what you will with me, Oh, my Jesus. I trust in you and you alone. The Lord blesses the righteous and dispels the wicked. Keep my Helen safe from all malefice and perfidy this night and always. Amen.

14

Jennie, 2020

Re: Third Miracle

Your Reverence,

I will get right to the third miracle, as my eye condition is worsening. This one involved a bike accident and six-year-old girl, Melissa Haighworth. Melissa was staying with her family in one of the rainbow cottages on the West side. This particular miracle is what resulted in the media coverage and letters and visitors to Old Lyme, Connecticut, for a chance to view and be healed by Jane Wright, or the "Guardian Angel" as quoted by Melissa Haighworth in the Old Lyme Gazette. Prior to the incident, Jane Wright's experiences, her healing and resurrection and even her stigmata wounds, were privately handled. She was unable to continue in public school, as she insisted on carrying her Bible and quoting scripture, which resulted in despicable bullying.

It happened this way: We were walking to the beach store on an errand for Eda. Melissa, the six-year-old, pedaled past us, unsteadily. It wasn't so uncommon to see little ones on their bikes. There were rarely any cars on Shoreline Drive; it was a friendly community. Everyone looked out for each other. Melissa was humming a song, the Sound wafting off her hair and clothes, sunburned cheeks, an oversized, dampened tee-shirt with a sunflower on the front and a hint of a blue bathing suit beneath, a faded moustache from some red drink. She was craning her neck, squinting. The sun was especially hot and bright that day. It was after a couple days of rain and it seemed to be ferocious upon its return, as if making up for lost time. Melissa put up a shaky hand in a friendly gesture as she pedaled past us. I recall being sightly nervous about her unsteadiness but also distracted by the five-dollar bill in my hand. After buying milk and a carton of eggs, we were told we could use the rest for ourselves. I had a honey dip donut on my mind. It was Sunday, mid-morning, and they came fresh from a kitchen in Clinton. My mouth waters just writing about it. The kitchen has been closed down now for some years.

At any rate, we were twenty yards or so away from the beach store, when Melissa began swerving back and forth, perhaps feeling more confident, and soon enough she wound up in the middle of the beach road. Before I could warn her, a blue truck came out of nowhere. Most drivers were cautious on our beach road, but this one was speeding. It happened so quickly. I heard the rattling engine, the horn, the screeching of tires and brakes, and then a horrifying silence. The kind that freezes you to the spot. I was numb, unable to move. Jane, on the other hand, rushed over to the front of the truck. I covered my face. I crouched down on side of the road. I wanted so badly to disappear. I don't know how long but it seemed a lifetime before Jane emerged. I was stunned when I saw her holding Melissa's hand. Despite a bit of blood on her cheek and a few cuts on her arms and knees, Melissa Haighworth appeared unscathed. Your Reverence, I felt an amazing sense of relief. I decided the truck must have missed her. I wasn't sure how, but the evidence was standing before me. If that wasn't enough of a miracle, when the truck driver came over to us, I realized a bigger miracle had occurred. The man looked as if he'd seen a ghost. He could barely talk. I assumed he must have been in shock from the scare. He just kept shaking his head back and forth, with his eyes fixed on the little girl. "How did that happen? I hit her. I tell you, I hit her! She flew about ten feet into the air. No lie. She landed right over there on the side of the road." Then he turned to Jane, seeking an answer. "What did you do?" he asked, more than once. I wondered what she'd say. Jane was quiet in the same way she was the day at the creek and the time she healed Eda. She just stared back at him, unaffected. The man looked at me, perplexed, as if for answers, and part of me felt badly for him. He couldn't understand how the girl wasn't dead. If it weren't for the creek and Eda, I might have been more shocked, too. "I hit her. I tell you I hit her straight on," he continued, and it was apparent he was disbelieving of what occurred. He knew it was too much impact for a young girl to endure, and Melissa Haighworth should have been deceased, not standing in front of us with a few minor cuts. Soon after, the ambulance and police arrived. And they were stymied. At one point, as much as I didn't want to see, we found ourselves in front of the truck. We saw the dented bumper and hood, the broken windshield, Melissa's Schwinn twisted and on its side six feet in front of the truck. I was convinced it was Jane who must have revived her. Melissa Haighworth was taken in the ambulance, despite minor injuries.

"It's a miracle," the driver of the truck said, and he was smiling with a look of wonderment on his face.

It hit the news fast. The next day it made headlines, *A Miracle in Old Lyme*. The driver of the truck, Jason Benson, was quoted as saying "It was nothing shy of a miracle . . . that girl flew at least ten feet," and Melissa described it as "An angel came to me like a bright light and whispered to me." She was talking about Jane, Your Reverence. Veteran, Tim Farrell, a paramedic, also contributed and added to being baffled. "With that kind of damage to the truck and the bike . . . it don't make sense."

Melissa Haighworth would go on to write the New York Times best seller, *My Guardian Angel*.

After the third miracle, I had no choice but to believe. And some part of me was petrified by it all.

And now, I apologize, but Maribel is knocking with my tea and medicine, and I'm a bit drained from recollecting the incident. It was so profound for me that I actually have exhausted myself, emotionally and physically. I pray my descriptions are thorough and specific enough to sound believable and to touch you in some way as well.

Your loyal servant in Christ,
Jennie Wright.

Re: Helen

Dear Bishop Monroe,

I am past the halfway mark and my endeavor will end shortly. For these reasons, I want to discuss with you more about Helen, the sweet child born to Jane Wright. It's apparent how much Jane loved her daughter. The greatest tragedy was our disbelief in her lucidity. I agreed to raise Helen and she was surrounded by love and nurturing. John convinced me Jane was not coherent and able to raise her, so I stepped in. It was shortly after Helen was born and Jane was sent to Mother of Mercy Home for Women, which would be her home, until her death nineteen years later. Soon after, I received a letter from my brother describing his predicament. He was going overseas to practice medicine, awarded a prestigious grant to study one of his specialty areas in genetics. No one would deny John had a brilliant mind, but I know now there are limits to what we should know with regards to knowledge. Tragically, he died at a young age, shortly after Jane. Undoubtedly, there is a much higher power at work, one that requires our utmost attention, one that is immeasurably divine and higher than all of us, more powerful than the brightest of minds. If it's not recognized, and we pursue other aspirations for secular purposes, our pursuits are bound to fail in ways, result in misery and despair and unethical consequences. For John, he hid behind his career, failed to establish a true relationship with his daughter, his beloved wife's daughter. The two shared many traits. And then he was taken from this world too soon, according to God's plan, and was never able to make amends.

I'm sure, Your Excellency, all of what I'm writing is familiar. As you know, even the best of us are sinfully fallible. We turn away from God in pursuit of career, wealth, fame, only to suffer from a hubris, which diminishes and darkens our souls. Failing to seek God's help, or attribute any of our gifts to our holy Father, is a grave tragedy that is growing more prevalent in our decadent society. We consume and consume and tend to lose all sight of our true purpose. Great leaders and those of creative ingenuity who have made their mark on society, many of them, fail to realize in all things God works in mysterious ways and we never are to lose sight of it. So many avoid God altogether, and go on experiencing life's joys and sorrows and never consider God's part in it.

But I digress.

I agreed to take Helen, Your Excellency. I never hesitated. I do think I could have done better for her. Maxwell was on board, initially, but then his patience was tried and he missed his freedoms and the sea, and when he felt this unexpected parenthood was impeding his lifestyle, similar to John, he broke off our long engagement. I moved back to the cottage with Helen and Maribel, and he'd return periodically but it was never a long stay. John tried his best to spend time with Jane, but, unfortunately, it was infrequent. And it proved to be more harmful for him to see her, as poor Helen felt a deep sorrow when he left. As I alluded to above, the whole episode with Jane scared John and kept him away. I think he would have been a devoted and caring father had he not been so ambitious. Also, some part of him was reluctant to accept that Jane was beyond his understanding, beyond the realm of his science and research. One can strive too high, desire to know too much, as mentioned earlier. I'm reminded of Solomon's temple, his gold and wealth, his wives. It started with wisdom and he didn't stop there. Even God knew he went too far. We are all guilty of it, getting stuck on earthly pleasures and wanting more. Take me, for instance, I, too, desired my earthly pleasures above all else, Maxwell, the sea, the white sands, the lush life. I paid dearly for it. I lost sight of God, the divine, the creator. It is easy to lose sight of our purpose. Even the best of us take our eyes off God, turn away from the good truth, the Word. For me now it penetrates deeply into my soul, and I am nothing without it.

I've written enough. My eyes are sore and my hand is weak.
Until tomorrow . . . God willing.
Yours faithfully,
Jennifer Wright

15

Jane, 1950

October 5

EDA IS TOO SICK with her lung ailment to climb stairs. John told me she's healing but said she won't hold the baby until she's better. If I could see her, talk to her, inquire about you. Am I writing in vain? Oh, Jennie! Too much time has passed. Where are you? I've confronted the reality that Eda might never hold her granddaughter, and you may never read this, and that I might never see you again! Even that doesn't stop me. No, the writing sustains me. The time between feedings stretches out in long, indeterminate moments of insufferable loneliness and worry. I am tempted to get up and go to the bookshelf, retrieve Bonaventure and Faustina and St. John. Maybe there's more. Maybe a bible. It would be easy enough. I'm tempted, but some part of me is paralyzed by the deceit, tortured by a strange reluctance. I crave John's permission, his affirmation. And to think how elated I felt to return to Faustina's diary. I broke out into tears. It was like finding my soul! But when I tried to read it, I had to stop, as I felt a deep sense of loss, as if I were mourning the past, or attempting to retrieve a previous time, a time when I was younger, and devoted, before this time, before my marriage and pregnancy. I don't know how I can return to that time, or if I should, or if I want to. I don't hear it in my inner soul like I once did. At one point, I became distraught. I threw Faustina to the ground. John happened to come in at the precise moment I was having my fit. Distressed, he picked it up and returned it to the bookshelf. "See?" he'd said, "It's unhealthy for you, Jane."

And when he left, my heart broke.

Days are long up here, and I feel a heaviness, as if a storm cloud has settled above me, permanently. During Faustina's darkest time, when she was a novitiate, prior to her vows, she suffered from a loss of faith. I wonder if she felt abandoned by Jesus when she could no longer decipher his words, or think clearly. Her writings suggest it. I relate so well to Faustina's confusion, her suffering and anguish. But now she's filed away, returned to the bookshelf.

And maybe it is best. I'm a wife. I'm a mother. I should devote my mind to these new roles of mine. I should suffer my trials, be patient and calm and coherent. If the visions return, or if I pray too much, and turn my devotions solely to God, John will suspect. He may turn away from me, decide I'm sick, or deluded. I should remember Faustina, how she suffered a similar treatment. She was the most conflicted when she wasn't taken seriously. When Mother Superior, or her confessor, didn't understand the depths of her faith, they concluded she was suffering from hallucinations. At one point she was told she was in no way saintly enough to have Jesus speak to her directly. Jesus came to me, spoke to me—before. I was chosen, holier, faithful. Now I'm not so certain what I am. John wants me his way.

I'm lost, Jennie, craving things inaccessible to me. And if I meditate too much on myself, dredge up the past, I become vain, self-indulgent. I need to put John and Helen first, in my thoughts and actions, and above all else. Oh, Lord! Rebuke me not! Heal me! My bones are vexed!

How will I do it? How will I protect my daughter? How will I ever help my sweet, sweet Helen, when I can barely help myself, or trust God's will, even though I know God's will is the only one that is right and pure? How do I insist Helen trust in a realm that is unearthly and incomprehensible to her? Do I believe it? Oh,

Jennie, I pray these words reach you! If you were here, you'd give me the perspective and strength I need. I'm weak-minded and unsure of my own beliefs. Maybe Helen deserves better. What will I do to protect her? Bullies will surround her, tease and even assault her. She'll need to forgive even the worst of people, the vile, the torturers, those who despise her. She'll need to walk in their shoes, see beneath the cruelty, accept all as one of God's creatures. If not me, who will tell her? Will she believe it in her heart and soul? Beneath one's earthly skin is the Holy Spirit working within and taking residence. Jesus was all things to all people, interacted with Samaritans, like the woman at the well, when he asked her for water, and there was the renewal, a lifting of the earthly veil. Jesus preached that material was secondary to the richness of God, the living water of life, which quenched eternal thirst. Nourishment comes not from food but from God alone. We cannot live by bread alone but by the word, and not partially but wholly. It is the truth beyond any truth accessible to us in our earthly ways of understanding.

Yes, it returns, Jennie! I was chosen for a divine purpose. My inner soul spoke to me. I'll tell Helen. God will arm me with the right words to make her believe me. I'll speak with conviction, and with God's armor, like Moses and his, mother, Jochebed, and King David, and Esther, and the other great leaders and followers of God's word. Helen, she too, will need to be strong, heavily armed in order to go up against the powers and principalities, against the rulers of darkness, the apostates and temptations.

I hear it. I smell it and sense its power. Behind this attic wall is the culmination of these ills, stewing at my emergence, my return to my God. Is it no wonder so many have succumbed to materialism and faithlessness? It is not an easy path, the path of righteousness, the one least traveled. It shakes all perception, takes great discernment and sacrifice. It requires firm conviction and unwavering devotion, beyond earthly pleasures. What appears to some is not so. Jesus offers the truth, lifts the veil from our eyes, as he did for the Samaritan at the well, and through God's anointment is the purity of the Holy Spirit.

I imbibe it now, the stirring of the Holy Spirit, as I write these words. I feel it working through me, an inner strength moves me. Once again, Jennie! Jesus speaks to me!

And now, finally, God is merciful! And my prayers are answered! I hear the creaking, the voices, John and Maribel, at the bottom of the stairs, and the sweet, small cries, which make me flush and my heart race, just to know she's near. And I'm proud of myself, Jennie. The sheet remains securely tacked up over the wallpaper.

I'm renewed!

3 a.m.

I could no longer hesitate. I thought of how the soul struggles. I weary with groaning. How a heart aches, turns so swiftly to the dark path. My new perceptions propelled me to get out of bed and walk over to the bookshelf, even in my weakened state, to retrieve Faustina's diary. My soul thirsts once again, thirsts for inner sanctification. I'm frail, easy prey for the invisible darkness. Oh, Lord my God, I prayed, in thee do I put my trust!

Here is what transpired: I felt such relief with Helen in my arms, but it was a brief moment. I can't hide it behind a sheet. And I know now it is not so much for me, but for my dear Helen's soul that I seek cleansing. My sweet Helen, initially, she fed so well, and fit perfectly in my arms. A peace overwhelmed me, like none that I recall, and then, something, some heavy presence, feasted itself onto her and worked its way into the purest interiors of her essence. I could see it in her eyes, the way they popped open from their quiet slumber, and took on a look of fear. That one so small and inexperienced could know such fear baffles me. But it was evident in her countenance, Jennie, and it made me shudder. I thought I was clever in covering up the wallpaper. I was not clever at all. But I was foolish to think I could eliminate the darkness. It's sinister and merciless, in the way it seeps through cracks and crevices, seeks to assault one's soul, penetrate and stick there, boring, infesting. Helen felt it. She reacted to it. I should have known. I should have prayed more! No, instead, as Maribel was placing her into my arms, I happened to glance over at the sheet. Maribel caught my gaze and inquired. I told her there was a draft coming from a crack in the wall. I feared she might remove it. I think she would have if not for Helen who started to whimper, thankfully, and it distracted. She placed Helen into my arms and my heart softened. But after she left, although I was relieved, some force compelled me to look at the sheet, and that's when I noticed it move, ever so slightly, as if a faint breeze caught it. I attributed it to the door shutting and fixed my eyes on Helen who had settled into feeding. I was completely hypnotized, enamored by her soft, rounded cheeks, her tiny fingers, the downy tuft of hair on her head, the translucent skin and tiny veins carrying fresh, rich blood. My beautiful Helen, I muttered, and she seemed to purr with delight. All seemed well in the attic in that one moment, which felt like pure unadulterated bliss—all trickery! I'm not so sure anymore what prompted me, whether it was a sound or a slight brush of air, but once again, I was drawn to the sheet. And this time it was undeniable, the way it blew outward, billowed as from some invisible gust of air. Helen, those eyes, the way she senses it. The purest of us are most vulnerable. My poor Helen. Jennie, if only you could be here with us, you'd strengthen my reserves. We are easy prey. Why would the sheet billow out in such a way if not for some dark force behind the wall? And haven't I suspected it, been captivated by the allure of it, even when we were young and it wasn't peeling quite as much, and it wasn't so dingy or decrepit? You wanted to poke at it and peel it. But I found the pattern immersive, perplexing. I'd trail my finger along it, tracing the path of the vines, here and there, and it held some kind of addicting mystique, bewitching, dizzying. You'd hit my hand away, tell me to focus. Yes, now I remember well how I'd lose myself in the labyrinth. I'd try to distinguish between the beginning and the end, apply some logical organization to it where there was none. It circled in upon itself. The conflict consumed me. Unlike you, Jennie. You were able to poke at it, indifferently, peel it, take control of it. I wanted to avoid it, but it lured me in, away from all sentience, all thoughts of purity and goodness.

Now the pattern has a stronghold, consumes like an invisible entity, a phantom only perceived through the senses, and it pricks my skin, and crawls up my spine, but I can't quite grasp it in a tangible manner.

I return to the holy, Faustina's words, her mind, her soul, to diminish the impending darkness infiltrating my soul. I kiss it, hold it close to my chest, having memorized much of it. I want to infuse it, drink from it, saturate myself with the divine words. I know it's a trial. I know how the soul tries, it tries and tries to purify itself with the divine, with the holiest of ways, but it falls short. God knows how much the soul can take. God's will protects and allows for our escape from this prison, just as Peter and Jeremiah were imprisoned and set free by God's will. I can't consider any other plan beyond what God has in store for us. His presence is ever stronger these times.

Yet I shrink at the sight of the wallpaper. If not for the hideous wallpaper, I'd be fine. A mere distraction, you'd call it, Jennie, if you were here to console me. And if I should tell someone, if I should try to confess to a priest or to the sisters, I'd be told it was God's grace, these trials. And I should remember what I endured—the wounds, the visions, Jesus' voice in my soul speaking to me, nudging me, appearing to me. I turned away to the flesh, to desire, to marriage, and abandoned my God, his plan for me. Is that what happened? The paper flutters, reminds me, a thorn pricking me, my broken cistern, my shameful iniquities, blazing, exposing, glaring back at me with unholy eyes of fire.

Jennie, I pray you hear these words in your soul.

Yes, I trust in you, Jesus. Find me in these drab corners of my room. I know now, the way of it, how external things surrounding me pale against the purest love, and are nothing at all. The purest of love cuts through the thickness of it, the divinity of God's love about me, the access to all places where death itself bows its head before it. Is this trickery or true goodness? Oh, even when I drift off into bliss, shortly, multiple torments press in on me. Let me envision Faustina's desire to be a violet hidden in in the grass, unfeeling of the feet treading upon it, continuing with itself and sharing its fragrance. Let me be ridiculed, shamed, spit upon, let my limbs be stretched beyond capacity, so that I might suffer our Savior's pain and take on the burden of sin as recompense for all our offences. Amen.

16

Jennie, 2020

Re: Fourth Miracle

DEAR BISHOP MONROE,

I want to now move onto the fourth miracle, the healing of Evan Ward.

He was a small, lovely boy. Jane took to him right away. She felt a deep sadness for him, despite Evan's cheerful temperament. Evan's parents would bring him down to the edge of the water as he was paralyzed and could not walk. He'd told us it was from a virus he contracted as a toddler. One might think he'd be bitter and angry, or at least envious of those who are healthy and agile, but not so with Evan who was a charming boy, who loved to laugh and tell stories. He had an amazing imagination. Jane, especially, was drawn to him. She'd sit by his side for hours, refusing to leave his side. She told me it was wrong to leave him alone. She'd later tell me her inner voice told her she needed to stay close to him and pray for him. Of course, I'm not so sure Evan was aware Jane was attempting to heal him, and, if he were, he might have scoffed at it. Eventually, there was less laughing and more somber, quiet murmuring between the two, which I know now was a kind of communal prayer. At one point, I recall glancing over and seeing the two holding hands. Admittedly, I became jealous and even resented Evan Ward, despite his frailty, as I blamed him for taking my best friend away from me. If not for him, she'd be with me, I'd thought. I took to pouting and scowling that summer. Stayed in a foul mood. I refused food and walked about shuffling my feet, arms folded, head down. Still, I was ignored, and they carried on with their conversations. Secretly I'd say my own prayers, which were contrary to Jane's prayers of miraculous healing. Mine were full of malice. That particular summer a flu was rampant and so I'd pray Evan might come down with it, so I'd have my Jane back. I often think back to it and feel a deep shame for these greedy desires. I was not completely convinced of my faith and applied it to my life loosely. I was immersed in the carnal pleasures and couldn't see beyond my comforts. Jane is the one who changed my mind, and made me a true and devout believer. But it took much time before that happened.

The healing of Evan Ward was yet another miracle and stronger evidence of Jane's sainthood, which brought me closer to accepting my faith.

It was on the final day Jane was to return home. To our shock, Evan was standing alone and upright at our doorstep, with only a cane to lean on. I almost fainted. Jane, on the other hand, dropped her suitcase and walked over to him and hugged him as if it were expected. "Look what you did! It's a miracle," he'd said. And then I heard quieter conversing between the two—Evan saying, "It worked" and then Jane's reply, "The Lord is merciful." And that was that.

I wasn't so sure of what happened. Eda, too, was flabbergasted. She shook her back and forth, and said, finally, "The Lord works in mysterious ways." Evan's parents stood at the edge of the property. Evan's mother had her hands up to her mouth, aghast, supported by Mr. Ward. I could tell they were both in disbelief and quite emotional. Afterwards, when I'd asked Jane what she'd felt happened, she told me to pray for an answer as only God knows. I think now maybe she was surprised herself, fearful of her own divine abilities.

So, Your Reverence, I complete the third miracle in timely fashion as my hand weakens and my sight is too blurry to continue and Maribel waits patiently across from me in the armchair.

Yours Faithfully,
Jennifer Wright

17

Jane, 1950

October 6

I WAS FEEDING HELEN last night, and I drifted off to sleep. I woke to a shifting of air, a dark stirring. I screamed out and poor Helen, the look on her face, the wide-eyes and scared expression, were too much for my heart to bear. Her tears pierced my soul. Just to think it was all my doing, that I could be so selfish as to startle my dear daughter. What is ailing my mind that these evil imaginations could beset me so? I figured they'd subside, but they only increased during the feeding. Maribel rushed in, and she pried her out of my arms, insisting she take her, just for a bit, to soothe her. Imagine? As if her own mother meant her harm. I tried to explain but she wouldn't hear it. No, she wouldn't have it. I'm still trembling and am left alone with an indescribable loss. Her heat remained behind, so I embraced myself just to feel her warmth wrapping around me. And as I did it, I felt the apostate's mockery, a sick hubris, a dark spirit curdling in the depths of the cavernous spaces behind the wallpaper.

Oh, Jennie. I still pray for you to come to me. By now I should know it won't happen. But something in me makes me think you'll hear me, that my words will reach your soul. Some tiny compartment filled with a hope spurs me on.

My greatest fear is the loss of my Helen. Maribel took her, disgusted, as if she suspects. How could she possibly perceive this foreign entity, one that terrorizes and encompasses me, wakes me, lurks and waits for me to close my eyes and then manifests in my mind. How do I explain it to Maribel? or John? What will become of Helen if she is taken from me? How will she navigate our broken world? All we can do is trust our senses, our faculties, our faith in the good, so that we can detect the loathsome and decrepit, the things that creep and crawl, that latch on, burrow in secretly, unnoticed places, whose origins are from a decadent time.

Now the strips sway in strange motion, as if it knows what I write. How can it be when the window is nailed shut and there is no breeze? How does air move of its own accord? It is an invisible strangeness, illogical, disordered, of an apostate angel's nature, one that basks in the impurity of chaos.

I should rip the paper off. I should do it now. I should get to the source.

Oh, Lord, let the wickedness come to an end! If only I were strong enough. But I'm weak and shaking. And now, while I'm writing, I hear Helen's cries coming from somewhere . . . inside there? Does it have her? No! I can't think it! I need to empty my mind, remain unthinking, lest my imaginings take hold. Oh, Jennie, I pray the soul-driven purpose of these words reach you and like a prayer of sorts, with the urgency intended, and inebriated with the divine, pierce your soul, and compel you to sail home.

18

Jennie, 2020

Darkness Afoot: The Exorcism

Dear Bishop Monroe,

I find it increasingly difficult to write and have commissioned Maribel to dictate for me. She will begin tomorrow. I think I have one more entry in me. Maribel has agreed, reluctantly, as she feels a higher power preventing her from returning to those days of Jane's, what she refers to as, "illness." Try as I might to convince her of Jane's sainthood, Maribel will not be persuaded. She agreed, partly, due to her being under my charge, and her loyalty to me, after all these years. Another curious aspect, too, which she's just disclosed to me, Your Reverence, is her nightmare. Just this morning, I was startled awake by screams coming from Maribel's bedroom. I woke in a fright, not sure of what to do, too feeble to investigate with the urgency it required. I was close to dialing the authorities, when she appeared in my doorway, off kilter in ways, but unharmed, nonetheless, from what I could ascertain in my limited vision. She explained to me the horrid creature that assaulted her in her sleep. She is unable, even now, to expound upon it without becoming anxious, but the scare convinced her to assist me in my task. I pray that her Godly service to this endeavor will dispel ungodly creatures from her slumbering state.

As much as I empathize with Maribel, I'm thankful as the incident reminded me of a relevant experience, which I had forgotten but now recall. On this particular occasion, Jane very likely cast out an evil presence incarnated in one of our favorite cousins, Benjamin.

It was a sunny day, with a morning fog lifting, and we were hunting for sea-glass. Cups in hand, eyes peeled to the sand, we headed out. The fog had just about moved out. Enough so we could see a fishing boat, a Sunfish and a couple dinghies out past the jetty. We crossed the creek, as it was low tide, knowing we had a few hours before high tide came in and we'd be unable to cross. Bernice was wary, still shook up about Jane's drowning experience in the creek. In fact, I almost wanted to walk back with her, but Jane held her hand and calmed her the way she's able to do. Benjamin taunted her, strangely enough, and he kept on about it. He even made her cry, at one point. It was unusual as the two were thick as thieves. I was aghast at the way he treated her, but I'd chalked it up, as kids will do, to a bad mood, or an impending virus. Never did I expect that his behavior would worsen.

Your Reverence, I can barely return to that moment when events began to alter, so alarmingly, when our sweet and lighthearted Benjamin changed from moody to dangerous.

We had crossed the creek and began our trek onto the Mile Creek Beach Club and went on until we reached White Sands. By this time, Jane had found a few of the blue sea glass, so she was satisfied, although you'd never know it. She rarely expressed too much excitement about earthly matters, but I'd noted a slight smile had formed on her face. It was when I was bending down to pick up a turquoise piece, when I heard the screams. I had lost sight of twins, which happens on these outings when we are so immersed in our hunt. It's mostly uneventful, so when I heard the shrieking, my heart stopped. I turned back to find Benjamin pulling Bernice into the water. I wouldn't have made much of it, except it appeared to more aggressive than playful, and Bernice's screams, too, suggested something out of sorts. I'd considered a kind of retribution for some previous ill-doing of a childish nature. But it seemed unlikely. Bernice was up to her waist. I could tell by her expression and protests, it wasn't a prank. But I couldn't imagine the trigger as Benjamin was a reserved and shy boy, and could easily become abashed at the slightest infraction. Although, I rushed over to them, Jane, on the other hand, just stood there, unmoved. I yelled at her to help, but it was as if she were no longer coherent or part of the physical world. She was lost in one of her meditative states. I realized I needed to act, quickly, if I were to save Bernice. Adrenaline pumping, I shouted at Benjamin to stop. He turned to look at me, and what I saw will haunt me to this day. Benjamin's usual calm and placid expression was now distorted. The fair complexion was a crimson red, beyond a sunburn, and with what looked like oozing blisters. His mouth was slightly parted and he clenched his teeth like a rabid dog. White foam formed at the corners of his mouth. At one point, I even heard a low growling coming from inside of him. He looked straight at me, Your Reverence, and his eyes were filled with rage and malice. This was not the Benjamin I knew. No, this was a demonic entity bent on revenge or destruction of the vilest nature. My first inclination, admittedly, was to run to safety. But I knew Bernice was in trouble, and as Jane was no help, I had to fight this thing that had taken possession of Benjamin, no matter what. Premature at birth, and Benjamin being of similar weight and size to his petite sister, thankfully, I was at least two inches taller with more weight on me. And with an adrenaline urging me on, I managed to grab hold of the back of his shirt. All the while, I imagined myself like one of the apostolate warriors battling arch-enemies. It was a battle of wills, of good and evil. I could make out Bernice's arms thrashing and it boiled inside of me. His hands were on the top of her head, holding our dear Bernice under the water. I was successful in yanking him back just enough to unsettle him, and he lost his footing when a rogue wave broke on us. Bernice's head popped up and I heard her gasp. But then he steadied himself and returned to his task. At that point, I clawed at his arms and his shirt, so viciously, I ripped it from his back. I was relentless, unthwarted, doing whatever I could do so Bernice could escape her brother's monstrous grip. During this time, I continued to yell for Jane, realizing I needed her help if we were to save Bernice. But Jane remained immobile, standing at the edge of the water, head down, lips parted and moving, eyes closed, arms extended. Jane was praying. Forgive me for saying, Your Reverence, but I was not thankful but rather seethed with anger at the sight of her. Now is not the time for prayer, I'd thought, and I was livid. I demanded she help. I was faithless, frantic, and I needed her strength—her physical strength. I had no investment in her prayers at that point. I needed another set of arms and hands. I needed brute strength. Bernice had been down too long, and I was feeling defeated. My arms fell at my sides, and I collapsed from weakness. My will broke. She's gone, I'd decided. How could it be? Just a few minutes ago, we were collecting sea glass. And now this? What kind of God allows a boy to drown his own flesh and blood? And then just as I was ready to run for help, Benjamin let go of his grip on Bernice, and stumbled out of the water and onto the shore. He collapsed onto the sand. His arms thrashed and he appeared to be having some kind of a seizure. I rushed over to Bernice and grabbed her. I was able to pull her up out of the water and drag her to shore. Jane remained in the same spot, and continued to pray, eyes closed, hands extended. Benjamin continued to writhe. His eyes rolled into the back of his head. He was on the sand convulsing. Meanwhile, Bernice woke and coughed up water. She was alive and now the tides had turned, and I was sure her brother was dying. Your Reverence, I didn't know what to make of it all. When I witnessed the transformation—Benjamin's mouth settle, his lips return to their flushed state, the oozing blisters disappear, and his docile expression return—I realized it had to be God's doing. Jane's praying was necessary. She had exorcised a dark entity from Benjamin. And Bernice was forgiving of her brother, as if she knew. She stood up and rushed over to him, held his head in her arms. He woke, instantly, and looked up at her, and never did I encounter such an intense moment of love, Your Reverence. It moved over us all. Jane was on her knees, head bowed, depleted of all energies. I called out to her and this time she turned around and looked right at me. Her eyes glittered, and a light shone about her head like a halo, and I heard her mutter, softly, "Praise God." I held her and we both cried and cried until there were no tears left in our innocent eyes. Benjamin and Bernice looked on, confused as to what happened. How could I utter it? There were no words to describe what I witnessed. I encountered the dark powers battling the good. I witnessed the power of God's apostolate warriors, the power of prayer, Jane's prayers, which cast out the demon from Benjamin, and saved Bernice, and my heart raced in my chest for Jane, for God, for all the sacrifices of his son's suffering to protect us from sin. And still it moves about us, lurks in well-lit rooms, tricks, and deceives.

I'll end here, Your Reverence, as the page is blurry, wet from tears, and my soul aches for rest and regeneration.

Yours in Christ,

Jennie Wright

19

Jane, 1950

October 7

OH, JENNIE! WITH EACH passing day, I wonder when you'll return. The days and nights stretch out, interminably, before me. And to make matters worse, Maribel was a bearer of bad news. First, she said Eda had a relapse and would have to return to the hospital. Then she went on about the storms in the Pacific. She left me alone to imagine our poor, Eda, suffering, and you being tossed about in hurricane winds and waves. Please don't fall in! I need you here! I need to tell you my fears, how much I miss my sweet, sweet Helen. I hear her cries in my sleep. I suspect someone is feeding her. I'm in pain, mental and physical, knowing if my milk dries up, I'll have nothing for her. Then what purpose do I serve? I yearn for freedom, for the ocean breeze, the sand on my feet. Save me! Save me from this prison, Jennie! I've sunk deep in the mire, imprisoned like Jeremiah in Malciah's dungeon, stuck for years waist deep in the mire. But then I stop myself from vanity and self-pity, knowing my limbs are free and unrestricted. And the sun beams in through the gable window, an array of colors to nourish me, even if some part of me rejects it, wants to turn away, knowing if I accept it wholly, I'll lose all constraint. John will know, and I'll be ostracized, sent away and forbidden from seeing Helen. Should a mother have to choose? Even our blessed Mother Mary was able to raise her son. Yet she was private and kept things in her heart. I should do the same. That's all I ask for is time with her, to instill in her goodness and faith. Is it selfish of me to love her too much, to cherish God's creation? I need to be with her. My arms are empty. I'm an empty vessel without her. When I asked Maribel, she had some sadness about her, like a secret she's keeping from me. A prison is not only physical. No, there is a mental prison. We can be trapped in a way of thinking, in a deceitful practice, in a lie, or mistruth, and we stick to it, and refuse to repent. I pray for Maribel. I know she's a good soul but she is fearful. She has vision but is blind to the truth. And I need to keep Helen out of the arms of all who have a dark malice in them. I know how it can infect a person, seep into their tiny souls. Oh, my dear Helen. I can't even think it. My page is soaked from tears. When will you come to me, Jennie? I've decided to insist John contact you and send you to me. I've no more patience for my situation. How easily a sorrow turns to rage. I could tear these journal pages to shreds. But I won't. For if I do, I might shred my last bits of hope and invite futility.

The paper is rustling. The air is still and yet it sways, ever so slightly. It is not a natural air. No. But another insidious source below the surface, one that hides and pounces, disguises itself in earthly costumes. I see it in my dreams now the way it traverses within the patterns, compassed about by a sickly yellow, a desperate flicker of light, weakened in ways, as if it would douse itself if it were able. The lines are sharply defined and bold like deep carvings, and they're sprawled out in optical horror as if piercing one's soul is the main intent. I can only imagine what is beneath, the malefactor. I know it is merely a trick of the eye. But when the sun casts a shadow on it, the forms take shape and emerge from behind it, friendly and inviting, oddly, but not to be trusted, as it melds and morphs and turns grotesque and hideous. Whatever entities hide beneath the wallpaper, Jennie. I must always be on the alert. If I tell John or Maribel, I will be sent away again and never see my Helen.

Now I hear Maribel on the stairs—

Update . . .

I demanded to know when I would see Helen. Maribel looked at me, strangely, with a sort of pity, the expression I recall too well, back when they sent me away, when the doctors compassed about me and sought to weaken my defenses, bore into my faith to disarm me, make me malleable, fixable. I can't bear it, Jennie. I just can't. I'd rather I cease to exist than be taken from my Helen, be placed where the people move about me half-alive, their souls drained. God wouldn't allow it. No, he must remember me, Jennie. I was one of his chosen, like David. When David was forced into a dark place, abandoned and destitute, God didn't abandon him. God armed him, rescued him. I, too, am here, alone, waiting for the entity behind the wallpaper to seize me. I need courage to pray, where once I immersed myself in prayer. Now I'm slipping down into the abyss, to that dark place St. John describes, to the dark night, where light is hidden, where the soul is purged of all senses and pleasures. Once I arrive, I'll lose all hope and all track of time, so that it will seem, for me, an eternal despair. That's what will need to happen if I'm to unite with my divine Father again. I'll need to descend to the darkness, return to the lowest realm of my being where the soul is emptied. I'm not there, Jennie. No, not yet, as I derive pleasure from my reading and writing and I crave the feel of my sweet Helen's cheek up against mine. No, I'm in no way detached from my earthly desires. My mind is fixed solely on Helen. Helen is mine and I want her. I pray, merciful Father, allow me to hold my baby, the holiest of gifts you bestowed on me, even if for a moment. If it's not your will to do so, then provide me some degree of comfort to endure these trials. Amen. Oh, Jennie . . . What will I do? You'd know. You'd tell me.

I hear the creaking of the stairs! I pray it's real!

20

Jennie, 2020

Re: Darkness Afoot continued . . .

Your Reverence,

I have endured a bit of a setback as of late. It's been some time since I've been able to write. Maribel will not be dictating as she is out of sorts. I must finish my task, despite my weakened state. My eyes are failing me and I can barely make out the page. In addition, I've been suffering some other ailments which are of an unknown origin. I do feel that the maladies are resulting from my lack of sleep. I've been having strange visions of dark entities and fear closing my eyes. Part of me suspects I'm being tested, as I'm delving into the matters, dredging up particulars of a divine and dark matter. Both Maribel and I are experiencing a battle within these walls. I refuse to stop my writing but will hasten it. Initially, Maribel would not allow me to return to it but now has acquiesced as long as I take breaks.

I'd like to continue my discussion on Benjamin's exorcism.

After the incident, when Benjamin recovered, he seemed changed, quieter and at times we'd find him alone and praying on rosary beads Jane had given him. Bernice, unaccustomed to her brother's newfound spirituality, questioned him, and taunted him.

John, too, my brother, he could be quite harsh as well, and some of it, I realize now, was due to fear. We were all on the threshold of some new understanding. It was clear to us, how could it not be, that Benjamin was possessed that day on the beach with an evil deity, which caused him to inflict harm on his treasured sister, Bernice. She, too, was stunned by it, but didn't resort to the praying like her brother. One time, I recall her saying in his defense, when John was poking fun of him, that he's afraid so that's why he talks to God to keep the bad away. I remember the look on John's face. He smirked but then there was an apprehension in his eyes. I knew it conflicted him and he was struggling in his own way to apply reason, to understand the logical aspect of those words. He witnessed the event, too, but he never talked about it. Jane, on the other hand, took to praying with him early mornings. I'd hear the bed springs, the sandy steps as Jane made the descent, and then the creaky door, and I'd go downstairs and peer out the porch window, watch the two of them meet on the jetty, walking to the end, one behind the other. They stayed there most the morning. I'd crawl back into my bed, heathen that I was, and fall back to sleep. Two hours later, I'd wake, and they'd still be there, until Eda insist they come in for breakfast. Jane's insistence on her faith was apparent and impacted anyone she was in contact with. She saved so many and turned their eyes to God. I'm a living example, although it took a bit longer for me.

Maribel has asked me to stop for a break, so as promised, I stop here.

Sincerely yours in Christ,
Jennie Wright

21

Jane, 1950

October 8

I FEEL AS IF I've taken a journey and returned, emptied, unable to pray, blocked from all access to divinity. Like St. John's dark night and purgation of the soul. The light ceases to exist if there is no visible object for to reflect off. So, too, a purging of the soul when it is stripped of all natural and spiritual desires and faculties, so that it is deceived into thinking there is no divine purging occurring. I'm void of divinity, abandoned like Job and David, all abandoned saints who cried out to God. Even Jesus in his final hours cried out. The greater the suffering, the greater the love. How does one rationalize that suffering is a joy and brings one closer to God? If you think of how much Jesus suffered for us, how he insisted we take up our cross and follow him, then there is the assumption we are to suffer like Jesus and it will bring us joy and closer to him. We are to avoid the "minor transgressions" or "little moths" which annoy and pester, attempt to destroy one's inner spiritual life, eat away at it, leaving behind tiny holes big enough for the darkness to enter. What the soul doesn't realize is that it's being prepped for the divine light, the divine sweetness, which is absent of all distractions, natural inclinations, annihilated of all natural preferences. It's not expected to be a pleasant feeling of comfort and contentment, I imagine. All else pales when measured with faith and the commandments. For the path is wide and easy for those who believe. I've struggled with heart wrenching thoughts, imaginations, strange desires and sins. Although it might appear to the outsider my environment is safe and pleasant enough, but the darkness lurks. And you're far from me, Jennie, the person I need most. If only I had constrained myself, trusted not in my own words but in Jesus' words. Maybe you'd have stayed behind. Some part of me feels your fear overcame you and so you escaped with Maxwell to get as far away as you could from me. Even though, I never harmed anyone. Only myself. My sweet Helen, no matter what happens, she will be loved. She will know how it feels to be nurtured and loved, unconditionally.

But what if she should fall prey to mysticism, to false prophets, or esoterism? How easy it happens. Jesus shared the spirit of truth and peace through interactions and good deeds. How much does it take out of a person to do good, to promote faith, charity and forgiveness? And still, we fall short of it

Why me? I ask it daily. Why was I chosen, Jennie? For whatever reason, I was given the power to heal. I accepted my mission. Jesus claimed purity flowed through him by way of God, the light of the world, and he risked everything to gather his sheep into the fold, to preach to the nonbelievers, denouncing their traditions and insisting God's commandments were paramount, knowing sacrifice is necessary in order to tap into the richer source of life, the abundance of wealth in God's divine realm. As I write this, my hand moves of its own accord, and I feel as I'm returning from a long arduous journey, exiled, and returning home. And still Helen is absent from my arms. While I wait for her, I keep my mind focused on what's right and true.

22

Jennie, 2020

Re: Stigmata and Jane's Final Summer

Dear Bishop Monroe,

Good morning, indeed. It's a fine day. My peace of mind is restored! The sun is shining so brightly, and although I can't make it outside today, due to a mild cold, I'm blessed with a bay window overlooking the Sound. A lovely view, as I can see the sun on the water, tiny silver beads of purity and bliss, like the Holy Spirit stirring inside of me. These moments, Jane is beside me, guiding my soul.

My time is limited, I suspect, so I will try to write more economically. I pray it will be enough for you to organize a committee to consider Jane Wright's canonization.

I want to now discuss Jane's stigmata. Perhaps you are aware, as it was investigated years back and all over the news. With technology today, a topic such as Jane's possible stigmata spreads quickly. Not so, back in 1945.

At any rate, Jane was never contacted by any local clergy or the Bishop, and no one cared to examine her wounds. Eda might be to blame, as she was very private and did not want the publicity. I believed it to be self-inflicted as that made the most sense to me. I wasn't a devout Catholic at the time, although we did attend church on Sunday, infrequently, I was not in any way deeply devoted or educated on the saints and cases of stigmata. Nevertheless, oh, the pain and agony for my dear Jennie, and for me, now, when I recall her experiences, I can't help but weep. She must have felt so alone in her suffering.

Writing on this topic has been difficult and I'm forced to take frequent breaks, Your Reverence, and retreat to the ocean just to revive myself. It's a great challenge, as you must be aware to preserve privacy. And in these cases, so many are seeking a sign from God, something to hold onto. Sadly, it became a side show of sorts with news reporters and radicals hungry for a story and hunting my poor Jane down. She was only fifteen or so at the time of her stigmata, and she could barely leave the house. As you know, in these more secular days, these rare occurrences are dismissed more readily by medical doctors or psychiatry, and it rarely ever bodes well for a saint in our modern era. Unfortunately, for Jennie's sake, she had to endure tremendous pain and anguish. It wasn't so much the stigmata wounds but how she was dismissed and even repelled by society, forced to leave school, evaluated by doctors, and even locked up for a time due to the fear she was suicidal and might take her own life. Jane was quiet and submitted. She prayed and seemed to crave the privacy. But when they tried to medicate her with a variety of psychotropics her body seized up, and so they took her off everything. It makes sense now as Jane was not psychotic or suicidal.

During it all, Jane's faith, I know now, Your Reverence, sustained her. She wanted very much to know what God wanted from her. She conveyed messages from angels and even Jesus appeared to her with his five wounds. She never did suffer all of Jesus' wounds. It was her palms that bled. She kept them bandaged. During the summer, when she came to visit, she was reluctant to leave the cottage. It was unbearable, being inside during those hot summer days. Finally, Eda bought her a pair of rubber gloves so she could go in the water. It seemed to help. I felt like I was getting my Jane back, and even the wounds were healing. But then she'd have a fitful night, and I'd hear her praying, quietly, and when she did this, admittedly, it disturbed me, Your Reverence. Please forgive me for saying. At the time, I wasn't so convinced about the whole Jesus thing. I wasn't much of a believer. I'm ashamed to say, fear gripped me. Maybe if I had more faith. Eda tried to instill in us the faith, but I'm afraid her inconsistency led us astray. And as we grew older, we stopped going to church. John proclaimed to be an atheist. I was more than likely an agnostic myself. Jane told me I needed to pray, and insisted we go to church. She said she prayed for our souls. She'd take my bike and ride there herself, not just on Sundays. During the summer when she had the wounds in her hands, she went daily. She'd leave at the crack of dawn and didn't return home until lunch time. She'd said she liked talking to God and that Jesus spoke to her. He told her she was to be a messenger. But then she was silent about it, which suggested to me it was a personal thing. I think it may have scared her as well. And she was conflicted, knowing Jane. She became obsessed with the Diary of St. Faustina. It was apparent how she was inspired. I believe she may have emulated Faustina. She'd confessed to me on a few occasions her fondness for Faustina and quoted the saint, frequently. The doctors said her wounds were psychosomatic, and believed it was Jane who somehow caused it. I'm sure you're familiar with stigmata, Your Reverence, and know that there are only a small number of stigmata cases the church recognizes. So, it's understandable that Jane's case would fall under the radar, or be dismissed. Eda didn't talk about it much with me. She became angry when reporters called her and tried to garner information. On a few occasions, she threatened to put Jane on the train and send her home for the summer. If you can imagine it, our cottage was swarming with journalists wanting to see Jane, to talk to her, to touch her. Eda Wright was a private woman so this was very difficult for her to endure. But she was also empathetic and felt sorrowful towards these ailing people who came to our cottage, young and old alike, who truly believed in the healing powers of our own, Jane Wright. It was a sight to behold, the sick lined up, some in wheelchairs, some on crutches, parents clutching their sick and crying children. It was tragic, and we weren't prepared for it. I think of Jesus, how he'd perform a miracle, and then tell the healed and the witnesses to it to keep it to themselves. Now I realize, he did this to avoid the backlash and tumult. Eda refused to open the door to these people. Although, some part of me believed we should have. I tried to talk to Jane about it, but she was silent and submissive. The one time she did speak about it, she told me they were harmless, only seeking a sign. When I asked if she thought we should allow them in, she'd said, yes of course. But she knew it was not her house, not her decision to make. If she wasn't too weak she'd go to them, instead, knowing Eda wouldn't budge on the topic. She sat with them in their tents, on the beach, or they'd walk with her on the jetty, if the weren't too frail. I felt she was vulnerable, in danger, even, of being kidnapped, or succumbing to mental exhaustion. I didn't know what to think. What if she wasn't in her right mind? At this point, she was depleted of all energy, especially, when her palms were bleeding. She became pale and anemic due to the loss of blood. Ruth stayed with us then. Both she and my mother were beside themselves, taking her from one specialist to another. She was prescribed sedatives and iron pills. She refused to take any medicines. She claimed Jesus was speaking to her through an angel of God. When she developed sores on her feet, it was worse, and she could barely move and became feverish and very ill. I feared she might succumb to her wounds, like Jesus. I prayed for her, any words that came to mind, anything to save my Jane. She'd only take a few sips of water, and despite her suffering, she'd begged us not to contact any more doctors. Eda and Ruth, desperate for answers, reached out to the local parish. Eda explained the situation to our priest at Saint Peter's, Father Moran. He was a new priest, fresh out of the seminary and wary of making waves, I realize now. He did agree to come to the house and bless it, and speak to Jane. But when he arrived, he could barely find a place to park, and when he got out of the car, he was engulfed by reporters with cameras, pleading with him for information, a story. We watched from the window. It was hard to believe our Jane could be causing such a disturbance. Father Moran was able to make it inside the cottage. He took pictures of Jane's wounds (see the enclosure). And he blessed the house. He refrained from any definitive remarks but said he'd present it to his superior for input. I am unsure of the outcome. Eda kept much to herself.

Maribel is here now. I need to take my rest. Strangely, a piercing ache in my palms and my feet has developed. Maybe not so strange. God works in mysterious ways.

Your loyal servant in Christ,
Jennie Wright

Re: Stigmata continued . . .

Most Reverent Sir,

Rested and energized, I begin with an urgency to continue my discussion from yesterday. I'm afraid we didn't handle Jane's stigmata very well, and we encouraged Jane to disobey God's will. It was meant for the others, the sick, the ones seeking a sign. Jane at one point refused to come out of her room and hid herself from the public, as if she were ashamed. I've been conflicted for a long time on this matter. And so I reach out to you in the hopes you will investigate further. I've included the photographs taken at the doctor's office and the reports. A neurologist hooked her up to a machine. She prayed and they recorded her brain activity. They discovered unusual activity in Jane's awake state. She was able to enter into the Delta state of mind. Usually this is evident when one is in a deep sleep. I also pray you will take into consideration all the other mysterious accounts I've included. Upon further thought, perhaps you are inundated with letters, those seeking veneration. You are closer to the divine than I can ever imagine, and you may have letters just like mine, with photographs of what could be of a divine nature, wounds that appear to be like Jesus' wounds; but how can one really know what is the truth? In Jane's case, she kept so private so that there isn't as much evidence to suggest it was authentic, unfortunately.

As I said, when the wounds appeared, she'd be bleeding quite a bit. She became pale and lethargic. It lasted for weeks.

She insisted on remaining in the bedroom with her prayer book and rosary beads. At one point, we were able to go to the beach and swim. I thought I had my Jennie back. She woke up with a big smile, palms out. John had just come bursting in the room at about the same time, and his jaw dropped. I'll never forget the look on his face. He loved Jane so much, even back then. He worried for her, and, so, to find her healed was like a miracle for him. We were not overly religious, nothing like Jane. John wasn't shy about his doubt and often talked about aliens, citing the pyramids and other constructions, which he claimed could not have been built without modern tools and machinery. Jane never argued, but she'd scold him about doubting God and his faith. She'd quote scripture or leave behind literature on the saints and apologetic writings. She'd use it as leverage. When he wanted to take the dinghy out, or go crabbing, or swimming, or ride bikes up to the ice-cream bar, she'd tell him she'd do it only after he read Mark or Luke, or a chapter out of Saint John of the Cross's Spirit Canticle, or a passage from one of her apologetic theologies. After her conversion, Jane refused to read anything that wasn't the Bible, or of a divine nature. She refused to read what she called "secular" material the school provided. Her mother was forced to hire a tutor for home study. Often she was not able to attend school, or she was unwilling due to the bullying and her refusal of the curriculum. She aspired to join a monastery but Eda would not hear of it. She said she had a calling and angels were visiting her and giving her messages, telling her she needed to follow God's plan for her. She never clearly established the plan. I'd later find journal entries with the supposed words of angels and even Jesus describing what she needed to do. I think of Faustina, and other young saints, who were given specific instructions, which they followed. Faustina wanted to join a convent and even went door to door knocking, until she found the Sisters of Our Lady of Mercy, as you must know. According to Eda, Jane's mother was convinced Jane was suffering from some psychological malady. At such a young age, she'd have needed her permission. And so her predicament went unnoticed, for the most part. It wasn't until the miracle with Melissa Haighworth that same summer, that Jane's miracles became public. I imagine it'd be viral if it happened today with our social media.

To sum up the issue of stigmata, I now believe, without a doubt, that my dearest friend, Jane Wright, was suffering the Passion, the wounds of our Lord, Jesus Christ. I hope the evidence before you in this account, along with photographs and her writings, will be enough to consider an in-depth investigation to determine, once and for all, Jane Wright's heroic virtuosity.

Your loyal servant in Christ,

Jennie Wright

Below is her entry on the stigmata which might shed some light on her mindset.

Jane's Journal Entry on Stigmata

July 25, 1965

My palms bleed. I know I'm suffering his wounds. I should be more afraid, but I want to suffer for sins, and I trust in Jesus. He speaks to me. Eda was kind and bandaged my hands, but I'm sad for her. Mom is arriving tomorrow. Poor Eda seems distressed. With the bandage, thankfully, I can write. But the bleeding continues and there's pain in my palms, and on my forehead too! I know it's from the crown of thorns. Oh, the pain Jesus must have endured, for hours and hours. I feel weakened but continue to pray for guidance. I'm sure it's a divine message for me, and I'm to suffer for sins in the way Faustina suffered. Faustina has helped me to understand. I thank God for her words. But Eda is already so concerned and I worry my mother will take me home. And there's no additional bleeding. It comes and goes in waves. Right now, I can barely get out of bed. I'm too weak to stand. Jennie seems mad at me. Maybe she thinks I'm ruining her summer. But more than that, she's afraid for me.

4 a.m.

I fell asleep and woke to Jesus standing over my bed. He wore a glimmering white robe with a gold sash girdled about his waist. A bright light engulfed him. I believed I was dreaming. I saw his wounds and tears of blood dripping down his cheeks. I felt his physical pain and sadness deep inside. He is guiding my hand so I can write. An inner voice said to suffer with him as a sign of his sacrifice. His words were inside me. I fell asleep reading Faustina's diary, so I can't help but think she infiltrated my dreams. Still, it doesn't explain how my palms bleed and the sharp pains in my forehead. I'm dying for Jesus. If that's what has to happen, I submit to it, just as Faustina and the other martyred saints submitted. All by his will not mine. Mom confuses me. She sat by my side all night, cooling my forehead with a washcloth, said I was feverish. When I told her I saw Jesus, she attributed it to the fever. She made me doubt. Was Jesus a delusion from my fever, or a real vision? Did I wake or was I dreaming? And who can I tell? Who will believe me? I keep these things in my heart. I trust in Jesus, pray to him to help me, to give me understanding. God alone, as Faustina said, can place one's soul teetering on the edge of a precipice and leave them there to flounder. With faith and obedience, I can rise above the darkness of doubts. I read about the saints to know my own soul. Bonaventure and Augustine and Faustina, especially, guide me. None of us are earthly creatures. We are here, temporarily, as a vapor, temporal creatures awaiting judgement. The less importance we place on earthly matters, the better we will be, the purer and more absolved. That's all I can say on it. For now my palms bleed and in my weakened state, when I suffer the Passion, I am closer to Jesus' suffering for us, for all that is holy. So I suffer for humanity, for mercy, and I embrace it.

Re: *Mother of Mercy Home*

Dear Bishop Monroe,

I regret to say that Maribel has taken a turn for the worst. After our last dictation, she admitted to feeling too weak to continue.

She later confessed, that she felt a deep remorse for her behavior. She, herself, had never established a connection to God and so to hear these events and write them down, caused a malaise of which she's never experienced. I feel as if she is at a crossroads and is rethinking her beliefs.

And then, by some strange turn of events, more than likely of a divine origin, I woke with a newfound energy, and I'm now able to see clearly. As Maribel's vigor declines, my strength appears to have increased. So I will continue on my own, until I am no longer able, with my accounts of Jane Wright.

You may be wondering how Jane wound up at Mother of Mercy Home, if she was deemed mentally unfit. Typically, in our modern day, those who have visions are hospitalized and diagnosed with a mental illness, such as schizophrenia, for instance, and prescribed powerful psychotropics. I will explain the circumstances leading up to her stay at the home.

Her stigmatic experience is what triggered the mental health authorities to get involved. For a whole summer, we kept her at the cottage and out of the public eye. We failed. Eventually, someone took note of her bleeding, and reported, anonymously, to the police, concerned that she was being abused and neglected. Next, came the required evaluation at the hospital. She'd already been observed and did a short stint at the hospital where a variety of tests were performed. As mentioned earlier on in my letters, a renowned neurologist was involved. He was intrigued with Jane's case. He hooked her up to a machine. She prayed and they recorded her brain activity and discovered unusual activity in her awake state. She was able to enter into the Delta state of mind. Father Perry was consulted, our local priest, to confirm some type of spiritual occurrence, but there was no conclusive data, or not enough, so she was placed on medications for depression and a possible psychosis. The medicines resulted in seizures and rare reactions, so she was taken off all psychotropics. She was considered an anomaly, and Father Perry wrote it up in a report, which is included with my writings, so you can review his thoughts on her wounds, along with images of the wounds in her palms and feet.

In short, Father Perry determined there was a similarity to other past stigmata incidents, and to quote him, "a possibility of a spiritual phenomenon based on JW's reoccurring wounds, which continue to reoccur, and lack a particular origin." Consequently, Jane was forced to stay under watch for weeks at a time, hospitalized. It must have been horrific for her. We have progressed in our humane treatment of the mentally ill, but back in the 40s, as I've mentioned in earlier entries, it was criminal how patients were treated. My poor Jane. I shudder to even imagine it. By the grace of God working through Father Perry, she was released. Due to her unusual circumstances, and the evidence of a possible stigmata, Father Perry was able to approve her stay at Mother of Mercy Home, while the investigation continued.

I was saddened beyond belief when I heard the news. Eda sat us all down and explained how Jane would not be spending the summer but staying at the home to heal. She said it was best for her and that the hospital was not a healing place. Although isolated and restricted, Jane was able to go to the chapel and pray with the sisters and felt safe and accepted in this setting. And she being one of the youngest, they looked out for her. She received all her schooling there as well. I remember the summer when she was released. I hadn't seen her in a few years. We were eighteen-years old at the time. She'd write letters to me, but she seemed so removed from the Jane I knew, so I had difficulty responding to her. I went on with my life. Most of her letters, too, were steeped in scriptures. I was at the age where I was concerned with boyfriends and first jobs and wearing makeup. Suffice it to say, I never believed it possible, but we moved on from each other. Tears flow from my eyes, even now, at the idea of it.

That's why when she did come to visit, upon her release, I didn't know what to expect. I was surprised to find, my soul, my sister, Jane had returned. She was the way I remembered her, way back, before the incident at the creek, when things changed. I decided the experience of being sent to Mother of Mercy Home, and being forced out of society those three years, made her crave more pleasures, rather than less. John was especially enamored by her. And the two were together all the time, so by the end of the summer, he'd proposed to her. At any rate, I had met my future husband, Maxwell, at the Old Lyme theater, and we were engaged that same summer. We were busy preparing to sail the South Pacific on his yacht. I was easily taken by this handsome sailor, loafer, Cornell graduate, who offered me wealth and earthly pleasures, which I now know were merely distractions away from the true purpose of the soul's journey. Still, I abandoned Jane, our simple Northeastern lifestyle, and left for the glamor of the exotic seas. I won't deny I'd experienced God's creation, firsthand, but I only realize, in hindsight, how much more I might have appreciated it had I been a true believer and not experienced it with a selfishly, myopic vision. I took it all in with a carnal soul. There was much beauty to be found, but I also encountered a profound poverty I'd never imagined could exist. I had many opportunities to help the suffering souls, and I felt it in my heart, but, instead, I stayed clear of those as Maxwell insisted it was dangerous to engage with the indigenous people, as he referred to them. So we stayed in lavish resorts and attended functions, cavorted with the tourists, like us, the rich and notable people, who were sinful and blind to the purpose of our existence, and I realized, too late, were not true friends. Most were adulterers and had young mistresses half their age, and Maxwell was unfaithful, as well. I turned a blind eye, although I knew it was occurring, I was like the others, fearful of losing wealth, prestige, superficial friends, and all I had acquired. Meanwhile, during these years, I cut myself off from the past and from Jane. I had missed an important part of my life, a time when Jane needed me most and was suffering, and I, too, suffered profoundly, within my soul.

But I've returned, repentant, and I pray this last endeavor of mine will work. I take my rest now as my eyes and soul tire.

Yours in Christ,

Jennie Wright

23

Jane, 1950

October 10

I PLACED THE SHEET back over the wallpaper. Even with the sheet, I worry about a thing gnawing its way through. I worry Jennie. I worry. I imagine the old wood beneath, softened by age, rotting in parts, bad energies eroding it over time, liquified and seeping out. Right? It could happen. It's a risk I can't ignore. But if I should say something, even utter my anxieties, I risk losing Helen, if I haven't already.

If I pray to the saints, to our Holiest Mother, to the archangels, to intercede for protection, I may find safety. Maybe it's too late. With the fluttering of the wallpaper, and the dark presence, maybe I'm done. I fear some part of me has lost my connection to the divine. It's as if my soul has been wounded, pierced too profoundly, and brought too low. And my suffering is not the right kind but more selfish, carnal, of the senses. For Faustina, and the saints whose souls are purged of distractions, who are worthy, suffering is neither feared nor rejected, but a wellspring of joy and immense relief to be in the arms of a loving Father, to feel one's soul lifted and purged and washed with grace is an unutterable calm not comprehended in an earthly manner. Faustina rarely loses the presence of God in her soul. She suffers and rejoices in him. I once knew him this way, that same intimacy. . .or so I thought. My doubt is manifested in the wallpaper, the wall behind it, the dark entities feasting off my doubt. The wallpaper blows insanely now, worse now, as if it intuits my desire for purity. Only prayers of a loving and true soul can draw from the divine, the well of goodness and truth. Dear God, if it be your will, lower me down into well of goodness and purity, wash me. Return Jennie to me. Return Helen to me, too, safe and sound. Amen.

24

Jennie, 2020

Re: Return to Mother of Mercy Home

Dear Bishop Monroe,

The sun is shining so brightly today! Praise God! It's a miracle that my eyes are healed. It must be Jane! I've prayed to Jane so many times and she's interceded on my behalf!

I want to discuss Jane's deterioration, triggered by a preoccupation with the wallpaper, which upon first utterance might sound innocuous. I'll remind you the cottage was first one on the street and erected in 1940 by my father, Dr. Taylor Wright, for his first wife, Suzette, who adored the ocean and wanted to stay close to her parents in Old Lyme. Suzette died, tragically, of a lung disease only a year later. My father then met our mother, Eda, at Sound View Beach, and they married and had John first, and then me shortly after. The wallpaper was the original. My Great Aunt Rose is the last one I recall to stay in the attic. I was told she was a recluse. Prior to that, it was a spare room for the guests or nannies that stayed on for the summer. At any rate, Jane became consumed with this old, vintage wallpaper, which, as you can imagine, was in disrepair. When we were kids we'd peel it in parts and run our fingers along the tendrils, which swirled in endless sloops. But at some point, she became fearful of it, repulsed even. She'd scold me, or hit my hand if I touched it, said I was tampering with it. I suggested we rip it off, and she screamed at me. She became superstitious, paranoid, acted as if it the paper were a contagion of sorts, or that we could be cursed should we change its composition. I'd laugh at the time, unaware of how seriously she was understanding it all. She'd talk of it as if it were a living entity, and even when we were kids there was the foreshadowing of what was to come. Why John wouldn't have just ripped it off and repapered it is beyond me. If I had been around, I would have insisted. Jane was in no state of mind to protest. She was ill, suffering from malaise, battling the forces of good and evil, while anticipating the birth of her baby. I should have been there for her. I should have comforted her as only I could do for Jane. John tried, I'm sure, but he was too harsh and unaffected when it came to matters of the emotions. He'd write me letters about her, and I'd imagine her troubled soul. Yet I was so far away, so engrossed in my own selfish and lavish lifestyle. And perhaps I did mention returning once or twice, but I was discouraged by John, as if my appearance would make matters worse, trigger further delusions. He'd have no choice but to return her to the hospital. She was in a precarious state. In the photographs he'd include the two, and Jane seemed perfectly content. So I rationalized staying away. When all the time she needed me, desperately. The poor soul suffered.

At any rate, it brings me to the point of the wallpaper, and Jane's preoccupation. I first heard of it in a letter from John. He was worried that she was fixating on the wallpaper. He'd offered to remove it or paint over it, but she became so distraught, to the point where he was leery of broaching the topic. She'd taken to covering it up with a sheet. Initially, I wanted to chuckle at the absurdity, recalling her fussing with me over touching it. But in subsequent letters, I became concerned, especially after this one incident John described. He had walked in on Jane during a feeding time, surprised to find the bed empty. He searched, frantically, even looking under the bed. Finally, he'd found her in the closet with Helen in her arms. She'd argued that Helen was perfectly fine and didn't mind and that it was a comfy spot for them. When he chastised her for it, she'd said the draft from behind the wallpaper was a risk for Helen's lungs and made it difficult to concentrate during feedings. She described it as a cold and eerie chill. And then at the end of the letter, and this is what alarmed me most, John asked me to return home to help with the baby. I knew then he was no longer comfortable leaving Helen with Jane, and Eda had become ill and too frail to even climb the stairs. And so the sad state of affairs began.

I returned shortly after the correspondence, and I took charge of sweet little Helen. I was anticipating a reunion with Jane, but when I arrived, as John arranged it, she had already been sent to Mother of Mercy Home in Maryland. I insisted on visiting her but was told it would take some time for her to become acclimated. I was deeply disappointed, Your Reverence, but I felt I could make reparations by taking care of her precious daughter. I agreed, of course, to take care of Helen. It was only to be temporary, but Jane stayed longer than we expected. And I became too attached to Helen to ever even conceive of leaving her. Helen had such a contagious smile and a mild temperament. I was the only mother she knew. Eda passed away a few months after Jane, only to be followed by her best friend and Jane's mother, Ruth. It was a dark time. Yet Helen, despite the circumstances, was always protected and grew up surrounded by love and nurturing. When Jane returned to the cottage for visits, it was agreed upon that Helen's welfare took precedence over all else. Therefore, no one was to discuss any details related to Jane's absence. Helen was told Jane was her biological mother, but it was understood that Jane was unable to care for her. When Helen was young, as children do, she easily accepted the situation, as she had bonded so well with me from infancy. Helen referred to her mother by her first name, Jane. Although she rarely saw her, Helen was especially fond of Jane and looked forward to her visits. She also wrote many letters to her mother. All seemed to be going smoothly, until shortly after Helen's fifteenth birthday, after a brief visit from her mother. Helen surprised us all when she demanded to know the truth, why her mother didn't raise her.

And then we were left trying to mitigate the damage caused by the secrecy. We tried to explain as best we could, as delicately as possible, and she seemed to understand, initially, but the unsaid stewed inside of her and, as teens will do, she rebelled.

Helen's academics took a dive, and she began mingling with the wrong crowd. I won't go into too much detail about those few years, but it was an extremely difficult time for us. If not for the grace of God, Helen might not be alive today. Despite recovering from her addiction, she never did seem to forgive me, or her father. She found a small, private college to pursue her art degree and, after rehab, and returning to finish her degree, she, too, found many occasions, like her father, to not make it home. During breaks, she'd say she was working on campus or going home with friends. I only wanted her safety and happiness, as any mother wants for their children. But there's this ache in me that yearns for the days prior to her addiction. I know the drugs contributed to her angst and indifference. But I was her mother in all manners of what that entails, and so, Your Reverence, it pains me to write this, as I've not heard from my Helen in so many years. The last I did hear from her, she'd had dropped out of college, a full scholarship mind you, and she was living in California with a young man named, Samuel. She'd found a job working at an art gallery. I pray for her soul daily, and I pray to her mother, Jane, to intercede. My dying wish is not only to see Helen, just one more time before I pass on to the Eternal Kingdom, but that she find her faith.

I go on and on about Jane's daughter so that you understand the fallout of her situation, and how it impacted so many. I should say it's God's doing and this is his will. But my heart grieves. If Helen could know the truth of her mother, she might forgive her. She was eighteen and drug free when Jane passed on to the Eternal Kingdom. But after Jane's death, we worried about Helen relapsing. She dipped into a deep sorrow and refused to eat. She spent her days moping around, or in her room in the refurbished attic. If she did emerge, she'd disappear on foot. I thought of Jane, how we spent hours walking up and down the beach hunting for sea glass. Just like her mother, Helen would be the one to find the two or three blue pieces. I saw so much of Jane in her, like the way her eyes twinkled when she smiled, and the sweet dimple in her left cheek. She was beyond perfect to me. Eda and Maribel adored her as well. She was an angel sent from above, a gift to us. And if only her mother could have known her better, spent more time with her, the troubles that were to come later . . . Well, it is not productive to return to the past in such a way, Your Reverence.

I am weary now and must take my rest.

Your loyal servant in Christ,

Jennie Wright

25

Jane, 1950

October 11

MY MOTHER IS TOO ill to make the trip to Connecticut. It makes me think she'll never meet her granddaughter. The darkness is spreading. Maribel seems changed. She hides her hair beneath a scarf. Her gaze is averted. She speaks to me in hushed tones. I think she fears me. What she really fears is the evil source behind the swath of wallpaper. It's saturating the perimeter of the room, spilling out into all corners. And this morning, I noticed the gable window is murky, as if from a dense fog outside, no colors, no glorious rays of light. When I inquired, Maribel said not to fret about those matters. Is it my soul? Am I simply ruined? Am I being forewarned like some presage? Once we were young, Jennie, unte-thered, unblemished. The air was clear and bright and breathable. I had you, always. Now I'm abandoned, left to crawl along the floors of this dark cavern. My only desire is to be with you, comforted, safe, away from the malevolence.

Now I hear the creaky stairs!

Update . . .

He brought her to me, Jennie! My sweet, sweet Helen! The air cleared of all negative energies! Her cheeks were flushed and her skin was soft as lamb's ears, and she smelled like the most fragrant flowers, roses or hyacinths come to mind. I'm convinced she's impervious to the evil energies. She was completely content in my arms, and latched on, immediately. My love for her is boundless, and it compelled me to speak my mind. Yes, Jennie. I confessed to John. I told him I was done with resting and was ready to come out of the attic. I explained my sudden change of heart, how I've had time to reflect and decided it can't be true, as I can't recall a fever or any kind of ailment that would be contagious enough to keep me from my baby. I was stalwart, unwavering, Jennie. I demanded to be closer to Helen. I did it, Jennie. And, to my delight, John agreed! When I finished my soul felt lighter. And even the window cleared and a ray of sun broke through the gable window in a splash of color, as if a power returned to me, a divinity manifesting. John even apologized, said he'd make sure Maribel was bringing Helen to me for feedings. And he even tacked the sheet up for me. He paused in the doorway, just before leaving, and he looked at me, as if he were seeing me in a new way, and even seemed to be wiping away a tear. His loves goes deeper than I can imagine. But I wonder what could be making him despondent. Maybe he'll have to dismiss Maribel.

8:30 a.m.

Update . . .

I couldn't wait any longer, Jennie. . .for you, or for John. I waited long enough. Maribel was in the laundry room. I swaddled Helen and I crept down the stairs and slipped out the side door. I stood at the water's edge, inebriated by salt air and soft winds, serenaded by the gentle cadence of light waves, until the weather turned. Gusts of wind moved over us and rough waters broke and soaked us. Not to worry. We are safe in the attic, now, armed, and ready for battle. Words can't articulate, Jennie, so I end here.

26

Helen, 2020

Dear Bishop Monroe,

I'm writing in response to the inquiry as it relates to my deceased mother, Jane Wright. As I understand it, an investigative committee has been formed to determine my mother's canonization. My letter, and any other relevant documents I'm able to offer, will be used for evidence. I've included as evidence my letters to her, along with some letters from her faithful followers. I hope it suffices.

Initially, I was reluctant to respond. But then my Aunt Jennie passed away, and my return to the Old Lyme cottage has made me reconsider. I confess I've lost touch with her, aside from a few sporadic emails back and forth. I've lived on the West coast for most of my life, selling my art, and married to the love of my life, Samuel. We had one son, our beloved, Timothy, who never did get to know his grandmother or Great-Aunt Jennie. He only knows through what I've told him. I do regret my absence and wish I'd visited the cottage more often. Aunt Jennie became very devoted and tried to involve herself in our lives, but I was wary, and kept my distance, fearful of what I didn't know. I lived a messy, liberal life, a life void of any formal religion. The more Aunt Jennie talked scripture, the more I cringed. Both Samuel and I were free-spirited, and felt a good heart and kindness went a long way, and it was enough. We frowned upon the hypocrisy of the church, and the damage of structured religion. Despite our viewpoints, Timothy, following in his grandmother's footsteps, surprised us when he announced his decision to study at the seminary and become a priest. We couldn't be prouder. I've come to realize the deep devotion of Timothy, just like his grandmother, Jane Wright. He'd uncovered much about his grandmother, intrigued by her, all her followers, the letters and articles, and writings, and I was unaware of it. He kept it all from me, believing I might criticize him or discourage it. Sadly, I admit I might have done so. At the time, I was content with my secular life and not ready to accept these truths.

At any rate, I will do my best to provide as much information regarding my mother, Jane Wright, keeping in mind the nature of the investigation and what it could mean.

I'll begin by saying ours was not a traditional mother daughter relationship, as I lived apart from Jane, and so I knew my mother more as a conjuring up of her in my mind. In other words, I had very few real physical interactions. Jane Wright came to visit on holidays or during the summer for a couple of weeks, but she was a quiet person and rarely spoke. But when she did, her words stuck with me. Upon further thought, Jane spoke to me in different ways, spiritually, I guess one might say. Jane's words were perpetually in my head. She stayed inside her room on the second floor, mostly, and kept to herself. Aunt Jennie explained how she liked the solitude. One time I do recall asking if she liked living cut off from the society at the Mother of Mercy Home, and she talked about the sisters, how much she adored them. "I'm always in good company," she'd said. I saw her differently then. She'd smiled and I loved how her eyes twinkled. I was convinced, then, she had a close relationship to Jesus. It's engrained in my memory, that one moment, because it was the first time I saw myself in her, as we share the same dimple. Aunt Jennie had always said we were similar in so many ways. I never saw it. No, not until that moment.

As for my father, Dr. John Wright, I rarely saw him either. We were estranged. I was told after my mother was sent away, he made himself scarce. Then he died of a heart attack, shortly after

Jane. Even before that, I was always left with an unsatiated longing for both parents, even though I was doted on, immensely, by both Aunt Jennie and Maribel, my loving nanny. I do think my father felt guilty. I discovered some of his letters to my mother and they were heart wrenching, filled with apologies and remorse.

More to the point, I was unaware of Jane Wright's abilities or spiritual gifts, aside from how she made me feel. I was always under the impression she had a depression or mental illness and that's why she was unable to care for me. All I have left now are her journals, which were kept from me, until now. These past days, reading through them, I've become extremely emotional. I find myself alarmed, jarred by the findings, as I'm discovering so much about my birth mother, astounding new information. I'm savoring every word so it's taking longer than it should.

Part of me believes her journal entries are indicative of any new mother, suffering from a postpartum psychosis. In this case, my father, a doctor, was able to diagnose her properly. I can't say I agree, or disagree. I guess I'm more neutral on the topic. As for her sainthood, I have never directly experienced any intercessions through her, personally. I've included my letters as evidence of my intrigue, and the impact Jane Wright had on me. I'll offer these to collaborate in support, or not, of my mother's extraordinary gifts, for lack of anything else to share. Believe me, I wish I did have more to offer.

Perhaps my letters, written back in the sixties, crucial developmental years for me, will shed some insight on the subject. Returning to them, I, too, am unearthing old feelings, the youthful me, my hopes and dreams, long since buried.

27

Letters, 1966 to 1969

September 22, 1966

DEAR JANE,

Thank you so much for the beautiful rosaries! I just love the aquamarine gems. Today, I noticed a woman next to us at the stoplight had hers hanging from the mirror. I don't know if that's blasphemous or not. But maybe it makes a person feel safer. Aunt Jennie discouraged it.

I researched how to pray on the beads and each time I do, I think of you! I don't think I have as close a relationship to Jesus, or Mother Mary, but I still try. I'm also not so sure I'm doing it right. I wonder if there's something I'm supposed to be feeling or thinking when I pray. Maybe I should go to church so I could ask the priest. Aunt Jennie and Max aren't exactly church goers. He prefers to sleep in on Sundays, when he's here. He comes and goes. And he drinks too much. Aunt Jennie complains about it and they end up arguing.

More reason why I love my attic bedroom. I don't have to hear their fighting. I feel safe in my own space. Aunt Jennie refurbished it so nicely for me. She told me how you two spent a lot of time in here. She showed me all the dress-up clothes in the steam trunk from Aunt Jennie's mother, Eda, and some letters from her father, Taylor Wright, to Eda, and some from your mother, Ruth, to Eda. They both died when I was only a few months old, Aunt Jennie told me, so I never met either of them! Ruth and Eda shared a bond just like you and Aunt Jennie. I feel a strange connection to you in the attic, Jane. I imagine you and Aunt Jennie parading around in the beaded fringe dresses, acting like flappers, with brooches and gaudy necklaces and clip-on earrings, scarves and long gloves, talking with accents. I'd always begged to sleep here, but Aunt Jennie told me I needed to wait until I was sixteen.

My worst fear is that I'll die and never have a best friend like yours. I have a few close friends, but not a soulmate like you and Aunt Jennie. She's never been able to talk about you without tearing up.

I wish you'd come visit soon! Don't worry about writing me back. I understand you don't have much time. But I'd love it if you did!

Yours truly,

Helen

October 25, 1966

Dear Jane,

Maybe it's a coincidence, but since moving into the attic, I've been having very weird dreams. I wake in the middle of the night and can't get back to sleep. I wonder if you might pray for me. I'm not sure what's causing my nightmares. Maybe some kind of negative energy. In one dream, bugs crawled out of the corner wall, millions it seemed, and covered the bookshelf. I tried to stop them but they got on me, and that's when I woke up screaming. I know you pray a lot so maybe you can pray for good vibes!

On a lighter note, I have a new friend. His name is Charles Ward. His father owns the cottage across from us, so I've known him for a long time. He doesn't actually know I like him that way. We're more like close friends, almost the best friend I never had. I remember Aunt Jennie's stories about how dad proposed to you in the tunnel, underneath the cottage. And then you ended up marrying each other! I wonder if you miss him. It seems like you two were in love! I'll admit, I do miss having a father. Unfortunately, I never see dad much at all. He's always away on speaking engagements, or with patients. Aunt Jennie says it's the price for being a brilliant doctor. Maybe I could marry Charles one day. I doubt it will happen. But his father is very interesting. He mutters quite a bit under his breath and walks with a cane. Aunt Jennie says he's a brilliant professor, a Pulitzer prize winner, and author of lots of books. He has wild hair and squints. Charles said he's blind in one eye, which explains it. He told me he knows you, and that you were one special lady, and that you healed him, whatever that means. When I told him that you were at the Mother of Mercy Home, he nodded and said, "Ah, I'm not surprised," as if he was privy to some secret. He said he speaks to you in his prayers and that he mentioned you in one of his books. All of these stories fascinate me, Jane! I want to talk to you about it. But I do understand and realize that you have obligations to your sisters and God, etc. Aunt Jennie tells me you might be visiting in July. I can't wait to see you. I truly want to know more about you, Jane.

Love,
Helen

November 2, 1966

Dear Jane,

I wanted to thank you for my prayer book! I keep it by my bedside and say a few prayers each morning and night. Unfortunately, I still have strange nightmares. But last night I said a few prayers before I fell asleep, and I actually slept through the night. I'm a bit self-conscious of praying and worry about Aunt Jennie catching me. I'm not sure what she'd think. Isn't that awful! I mean, I'm sixteen-years old, and I should be able to make my own decisions on these matters, right? And the praying makes me feel peaceful. And, honestly, I'm not so interested in becoming a nun, to no degree am I devoted like you. I'm more interested in art. I'd like to become a famous artist, selling my work to the rich and famous, only because it would get more visibility that way.

On another note, I have some news for you! Charles kissed me! It was the oddest sensation, Jane. I wasn't sure what to make of it. We were sharing a hamburger and french-fries at the Shake Shack in the center, and he got this look in his eye. He has the most amazing hazel eyes, by the way. And then he took my hand and pulled me into him and, we touched lips and, voila! I had my first kiss! My heart raced. I didn't know what to do with my arms, my hands, my eyes! I couldn't help but imagine you beneath the cottage, and what your first kiss must have felt like. I imagine when you returned that summer and dad proposed to you for real, how you must have felt! Dad had already graduated from college, and would be starting an internship, and you finished your studies in theology at the Mother of Mercy Home, according to Aunt Jennie. She told me she was planning her life with Maxwell. What a time it must have been. I so wish I were a fly on the wall back then. I wish I could know more about that summer, how it felt to come home and to be swept off your feet. Is that how it happened? I imagine dad must have been so amazingly in love with you, to have waited for you all those years. It's a love story I want for myself! I also can't help but wonder why you broke your vow with the sisters and decided to live a more traditional life. And then to return after having me. . . I want you to know, Jane, I've never blamed you for not raising me. I know that you couldn't help it. But I do wish I knew you better. Was it your choice to go away and live with the sisters? Or was it against your will? Whenever I'd ask Aunt Jennie about it, she'd start tearing up, or change the subject. I hope one day we can sit down and talk about it.

Love,
Helen

June 10, 1967

Dear Jane,

I'm sorry I haven't written to you in a while. I've been a bit under the weather. A bad place, Jane. As I hear you're ill, too, this might just be my final letter to you. I want to tell you that I treasure the cross you gave me. I wear it every day, even if I'm not much of a believer these days, if I ever was. And maybe I should be. Maybe I'm sinful, deserving of the bad that comes my way.

After my last letter to you, which was more hopeful, the nightmares increased and I could barely sleep. I took cough medicine with codeine in it just to get to sleep. At first it helped, but then it made me feel worse. I dream about the bugs. Other times I'm stuck in the marsh, or out at sea, and pursued by a dark malevolent creature. Each time, I wake sweating and unable to breathe. Aunt Jennie finally took me to a doctor. I had dark circles under my eyes and could barely sleep more than a few hours. The doctor prescribed sleeping pills. Those worked, temporarily. Eventually, I started dipping into Aunt Jennie's liquor cabinet, which is reserved for holidays or special occasions, as she doesn't drink. I mixed the alcohol with the pills, and, sadly, I became addicted. It's difficult for me to even write this to you, Jane. I feel horrible about it all. I'm in a bad place. I'm sure that might sadden you and I don't mean to. I'm trembling right now and can barely write. If you were able to be here with me and raise me, maybe I'd be a better person. I've missed out on knowing you, and I don't hate you for it, or anyone. I just feel abandoned in ways, and disappointed, I guess. I was hoping you'd come to visit but Aunt Jennie says you haven't been well and that makes me feel even worse, knowing I might never see you again, never get to talk to you and know you, and when I need you the most. Do I need to pray for my own salvation? Is that it? Maybe I'd be less fearful. Maybe it's that simple. Maybe I need to pray more. I wish you were here with me. I live in an unholy world, in a secular world with drugs and corrupt and greedy people who don't care about themselves, or their bodies, or God. It's a sad world, Jane, and I know I've become one of them, and I've taken a dark path. And I can't say I like it very much. But I don't know how to get back.

Amidst all the bad, I was accepted to an art college. Just today I got the letter! I should be elated, right? Then why am I more depressed? I think, partly, because of Aunt Jennie. Max left, and I feel guilty leaving her. I imagine she blames me for Max leaving. And maybe she's right. But I know (and you'd agree) he wasn't a good man. He'd been cheating on her for a long time. Maybe I can take some of the blame. I've been selfish and cruel in my behaviors. I could have gone to a priest to confess, and suppose I still can, but I have no plans to take that route. Not now, anyways. I don't know why I have such negative thoughts. I guess you might say I need to be saved. But in all honesty, things got dark when Charles moved away. I felt like I lost my closest friend, and my purpose. For some reason I had it in my head that I was living some parallel existence to yours, Jane. I realize now I was deceiving myself. It was all just a fantasy. I've never had a true close friend, not like you had, or your parents. You have always been conjured up in my mind. And one day, I had a revelation. I realized the truth, which is that I don't know you, Jane! You're a figment of my imagination!

The reality of it hit me hard. I sunk into a dark depression. Aunt Jennie became distraught. Her sweet Helen was a drug addict. She took me to counselor after counselor, but no one could help. They tried medications and those made me deathly ill. Aunt Jennie explained to the doctors how you had a toxic reaction to pharmaceuticals. I felt another incident of closeness with you, a similarity we shared, more evidence that we shared the same DNA, that I grew inside of you, that you were, indeed, my real mother. And this just exacerbated my grief. I felt so lost like pieces of my life were stolen from me. Jane, mother, mom, whoever you are, it saddens me that I never got to know you and still don't. When I was younger, all I had to do was to pray to reach you. I imitated what you did and tried to live a life you wanted for me, and I felt a sense of peace. But then it didn't work anymore. My life changed. I fell in love with Charles and tried to find fulfillment with him. I never waited for marriage. No, we did things that I'm sure you'd frown upon. And after he left me, my solace became alcohol or drugs. I hurt the people I loved the most, especially Aunt Jennie. I can't tell you how many times I offended her. I'd run off for weeks at a time. I even stole from her to buy more drugs.

November 22, 1968

Dear Jane,

I'm so glad I didn't mail this sad, sad letter, without the addendum, which is my GOOD NEWS! I finished rehab at Cliffside Malibu. I'm a new person! No more nightmares or drugs. I got my life back in order. I've been here five months and I'm heading off to college on full scholarship in the spring to get my degree in art. Please pray for me! I need to stay on the right path. I just don't know what that path will be. If only I could have known you better. If only I could be as devoted as you. I feel as if a stronger faith might have helped me. I don't know that I'll write to you anymore, or if you'll even read this letter. So many unknowns. I know that I love who I've imagined you to be.

Love your daughter,
Helen

August 22, 1968

Dear Jane,

It's been awhile, I'm sorry to say, since I last wrote to you. I've had to come to terms with the news about your illness and make sense of what I've discovered about you. But before I discuss my thoughts on it, I want to share that I'm with someone who is perfect for me. No, it's not Charles. But I realize we never truly know the path we're to take. It all unfolds in surprising ways! You'd say by God's will, or something along those lines.

Samuel is an artist like me, but he does it as a hobby. Of course he's very modest and refuses to believe his work is genius. I was halfway through a semester, when I decided to drop out of college, as it seemed to me to be a waste of time and money, and I wanted to devote more time to my art, and that's when I found

Samuel. I happened to stop by for a slice of pizza at a place called Joey's, and I noticed all the brilliant artwork on the walls. I commented on it, and it just so happened Samuel was clearing the table next to me and claimed ownership. I guess you could say, I fell in love with his art, first. That's how it started. He told me his father owns the restaurant and insisted on hanging his paintings. Life is so rich, Jane. We both have these dreams and goals and he makes me feel a renewed sense of purpose. Thankfully, I'm able to stay in San Francisco, for now, as I have the Wright family trust Aunt Jennie finally agreed to let me tap into. The cost of housing, even for a small apartment is close to three-hundred a month! Samuel lives with me and we split the rent. I've also been selling some of my paintings at the art gallery where I work as a receptionist. The owner liked my work and agreed to let me showcase some pieces in the gallery. I've already sold one! It just so happens to be the one I painted of the cottage, with you in it. I took a picture and am including it with the letter.

The best news is that I'm entirely clean. I can't see myself ever returning to that decadent lifestyle. And you'll like this: I pray every night, and do the rosary at least once a day. Samuel thinks I'm obsessed and borderline insane, but I try to explain to him that I very well could have saintly genes coursing through my blood, referring to you, Jane, of course.

And now to the other topic. First of all, I realize I treated my Aunt Jennie horribly and need to make amends. But now with the news about you in the paper, and your miracles, and some suggesting you are a saint, I can't say it hasn't been difficult. She's kept so much from me, so many secrets all these years! I should have been able to make my own decisions on the matter of you, Jane. I missed out on so much of your life and have had to hear second hand what happened to you as a child. I never even knew about the creek incident and how you were resurrected! What does it all mean, Jane? And then the healing of Eda and Evan Ward. I had to go to the library to search the archives. I found an entire section devoted to you, *Saint in Old Lyme*. I can barely absorb it all. I'm not sure what to think! I've never been a strong believer, but now with this new information, I have to rethink my earlier convictions, dispel the doubts I might have had. Did you really perform actual miracles? Could it be true? We have plenty of cults here in California with false prophets reinterpreting the gospel and spreading lies, or what they say is the "good word." But you had so many followers! Did people come to our cottage to be healed? Did you really die and return? Did you heal Charles Ward's father, Evan Ward, and make him walk again? It all makes sense then why Evan Ward was so fond of you. And then the story about Melissa Haighworth, who just happens to be a best-selling author of *My Guardian Angel*, and whose been on talk shows and claims you brought her back to life. She describes the bike incident when she was six-years old, how it felt to die, and how Jane Wright, God's messenger, showed up and brought her back to life.

If it is all true, then who am I? Should I be waiting for a divine message from above? Will I receive a visitor from heaven? What about my nightmares? Were those warnings for me to pray more? And why was it kept a secret from me? Maybe it's that I'm too sinful, too earthly. Maybe I'm not worthy enough. When I was old enough, I started asking questions. The responses I received from Aunt Jennie were always vague and terse. I was always told you were not able to care for me, but that you loved me "profoundly." I accepted it because I felt so loved and taken care of by Aunt Jennie and Maribel, that I didn't think I needed anything else. I was protected. And even my schooling, for the most part, was at an exclusive private school. I never felt cut off, or lacking. I lived a rich life, Jane.

Maybe knowledge isn't always a good thing. Now I 'm not sure what to think. I feel betrayed in ways. I feel as if I've missed out of something sacred and momentous. Maybe if I knew, I could have stayed on the right path, declined the drugs. Maybe I could have witnessed a miracle, or talked to you about it. Maybe you could have saved me from myself. Maybe you did!

As I write, I'm opening new channels of pain. I feel as if I'm purging myself of all that's built up over the years. I wonder if you're well enough to respond to me. I doubt it will happen, but I so need to hear from you. I'm baffled, unable to make sense of you, or anything at all anymore. I cling to Samuel. He's the only thing that makes sense to me. I almost wish I'd never read what I did. I would prefer to keep the original idea of you in my head. Now it's evolved into something else, ungraspable, and it rattles my beliefs, my values, my sense of self and identity, everything I've become is shaken to its core. Samuel tries to console me, as he's so caring and concerned. But there's little he can do.

I'm left unsettled, Jane.

I hope to hear from you. Although you're ill, If I am able to visit, I'd be willing to do that as well. I'll get on a plane tomorrow to sit down with you and talk about it. I deserve to hear the truth from you.

Your daughter,

Helen

October 15, 1968

Dear Jane,

I'm sorry to hear about your sickness. Aunt Jennie says you are not able to visit. But I'm pursuing the truth on my own. I met with Evan Ward. He took me into his study. I've never seen so many books. He was thrilled I'd come to visit and said I reminded him of you! He made us some tea. I asked him about you and he didn't seem in the least bit flustered. His eyes brightened up and he told me all about that summer, how you sat by his side and prayed with him. He said it was the first time he prayed. He said he changed that summer, and he became a follower of Christ. He had visions and heard voices that summer. Afterwards, too, it continued and he developed a closer relationship to his faith and God. Unfortunately, he couldn't save his wife, and she died from Parkinson's, but he realized, as he said, "It just wasn't to be and God's will is manifested in the suffering just as profoundly as in the healing. We can't always know," he'd said. He spoke so eloquently, and he had a great sense of humor, Jane! At one point, he did get teary-eyed when he was remembering that summer. He had such a fondness for you. He wanted to know all about you and I gave him a copy of the news article. As he read it, he teared up, and said he didn't doubt any of it.

I'm so glad I visited with him, Jane. Just talking to him convinced me about you, made me realize that you are more than I could have ever imagined. It's all I can think about. Samuel is frustrated and wants me to stop obsessing over it all and pay him more attention. He thinks it's all getting to me. But I assure him it's healing and making me more whole. I've also been thinking back to our visits, how you made such an impact on me, how I wanted to imitate you, felt an enormous peace come over me. It all makes sense now. The points in my life when I turned away from the good, when I lost faith and became hardened and angry and sinful. I didn't care about myself, or anyone. I wonder if it's too late to seek forgiveness. I know you'll forgive me. Aunt Jennie, too, has always forgiven me for anything I've done.

I want to say that I can hear you in my head, Jane. I understand you better now. That voice of conscience was you all along, a conduit to God, guiding me to the right path. Sometimes, I chose to ignore it. Those people, strangers, coming to our cottage, they were looking for you, waiting for you, coming from all over the state, after Melissa Haighworth's accident and her words about being brought back to life. I found some letters:

> Dear Sister Jane,
> I'm writing to thank you for answering my prayers. I have no signs of disease. The doctors are baffled. I know it was you, Jane. You touched me and healed me and prayed for me!
> God Bless,
> Sandy

> Dear Sister Jane,
> My brother found Jesus! All because of you, Sister Jane. God Bless you.
> Rebecca from Canada.

> Dear Sister Jane,

God guided me to you, Jane. I knew you'd help me. I prayed and prayed for you to intercede on my behalf. You were there for me. You came to me in my dreams. I drove 200 miles just to see you. When you held my hands and blessed me, I felt a rush of the Holy Spirit come over me! Praise God!

> *In Christ,*
> *Thomas*

Dear Sister Jane,

I hope you will pray for me. My mother moved out. I miss her. I don't think she's returning. I'm afraid she hates me. My dad has a girlfriend and no one seems to care that mom is gone. I don't think it's right, do you? I would come see you but I don't know how I'd get there. I might take a bus but I'd have to save up some babysitting money. Please write back to me soon!!!

> *Love,*
> *Diane from Minnesota*
> *P.S. I learned the rosary and pray all the time*

Jane, these letters still come on a daily basis!

Reading them and being here at the cottage reminds me of the visitors, all the strangers that came to the cottage; some were very ill, hungry for healing, coming to Old Lyme, seeking you to heal them, pray for them. I remember it now, those beautiful strangers. It returns to me so vividly. They knew when you'd be visiting. You'd stop whatever you were doing and greet them. Aunt Jennie was wary about letting them into the cottage, so you'd go outside to them. Then you'd pray with them, holding their hands. Aunt Jennie kept me busy, tried to distract, lest I get disturbed or fearful of you. I'd peek out the porch screen, and watch the procession onto the beach and down to the water. At the time, I thought you were cooling off, or swimming, but now I know you were baptizing them just like the disciples, given power by Christ and the Holy Spirit. If someone told me the truth, maybe I would have believed. Maybe I would have partaken, prayed with you. Why did Aunt Jennie keep you from me? Wasn't it a good thing? Why would she think I'd ever be disturbed? A child is innocent, closer to the good in many ways. From what I've read lately, to be spiritual minded one has to think like a child, with that same naivete in order to be a true disciple of Jesus. I don't know that I am there, yet. I don't know if I'm fully on board, but I am moving more towards the reality of my childhood, and you, Jane, as my mother and so much more than that, a healer for many. The evidence speaks for itself, your followers, your believers, the letters, the writings about you.

I'm blessed, so blessed and proud to call you my mother!

Your loving daughter,

Helen

December 23, 1968

Dear Jane,

It's been two months since I sent your letter, and I haven't heard back from you. I was hoping I would. I can't even think about celebrating Christmas. I worry now more than ever. I wrote to Aunt Jennie and insisted she provide me with all the newspaper articles about you. I'm so disgusted and saddened by what I've read, especially the ones referring to you as a fraud, mentally unfit, deluded, psychotic, arguing for your institutionalization. I couldn't' help but draw parallels to Jesus Christ and his persecution, and the apostles and martyred saints who were rejected for their beliefs, locked up, tortured and beheaded. Now I worry for you. I want to see you and will ask Aunt Jennie if it's possible. I'm sorry for any hurt or troubles I may have caused you over the years. I don't know how much Aunt Jennie shared with you regarding my atrocious behavior but I pray you forgive me. Maybe you healed me? Maybe it was you all along who prayed for me? You're truly a saint. And to think you were so unjustly accused seems unfathomable to me. What's wrong with people? How can they dispute the hard evidence? Now I wonder if all this contributed to your staying at the Mother of Mercy Home. Was it of your own volition? When I'd ask Aunt Jennie, she'd always say it was your calling. But now I wonder. The first stay there you were barely eleven-years old. I would think it'd be best for young adults, maybe eighteen or so, who have chosen that profession. By the time you returned (or were allowed to leave) your pivotal years of development were gone. I'd always been perplexed by it, and sensed there was more I wasn't privy to, and when I couldn't find the right answers, I felt abandoned, lost, took the dark path and escaped into drugs to numb the pain.

Jane, I support you!

Love,

Helen

February 10, 1969

Dear Jane,

I'm so glad I was able to see you! I don't know if you'll get this letter in time as I know you're dying. I've accepted it. I have vivid dreams about being with you in your room, holding your hand. We're always in the attic. And it seems to me there is a part of you I've always needed to know more about. I imagine myself one of the strangers, one of the lost souls who sought you out. I wanted to be them, and, instead, I was a different kind of stranger, kept from you, distanced, cut off from being near you.

I picked up the prayer book and started reading today. I might be seeking something more from you, a way to reach you, perhaps. Samuel is worried. He agreed to read the news articles. He even agreed to read Melissa Haighworth's book, but then he said he couldn't finish it. At least he's being a sport about it. I struggled to get through it myself. Much of her book is devoted to her Near-Death Experience with just a few chapters devoted to the actual accident, and you. I think we tend to lose sight of what's important. I do think anything can be exploited or embellished for the sake of profit or fame for all the wrong reasons. I don't know if that's the case with Melissa. Her book is a best seller and so I'm sure she's reaped the rewards and is wealthy from it. She earned her rewards, but they are not the right kinds of rewards.

I know with you, Jane, that's not true. You shied away from any notoriety. You suffered a true sacrifice of self and earthly desires. You devoted all your life to your faith to God, and the doctrine and

133

the sisters. If you could have, I know now, you would have raised me, but it was not to be.

I don't know if you'll ever read this letter. But if you do, please know that I know you loved me more than you could ever show. I always felt loved by you, even though we were apart, and that speaks volumes.

Your faithful daughter,
Helen

28

Helen, 2020

Dear Bishop Monroe,

That was my final letter. She was able to read it, according to Aunt Jennie. And she died that same night. When I asked about her illness, Aunt Jennie said she had a weak heart. She died peacefully in her sleep.

After returning to my letters, I've concluded that my mother, Jane Wright, was holier than I ever realized, and could have ever imagined. While writing this response to you, I've undergone a transformation, soul searching, and it pained me, at times, so I reached out to the community for guidance. As a result, I've received hundreds of emails and letters from people all over the country who want to share their experience with my mother, messages of healing and hope. Some recovered fully from terminal diseases. Others were able to walk and stop the pain medication they'd been taking, just after one visit with Jane Wright. I've included all these as evidence for the case of my mother, Jane Wright. I know it may seem as if I'm fickle, but you must understand that this has been quite a bit for me to digest.

I'll add that upon first arriving home to the empty cottage, I thought to stay in the attic. But the nightmares returned, so I took the downstairs bedroom. I encountered a few other strange occurrences as well. Maybe it's irrelevant but perhaps it could contribute to the investigation. I woke twice thinking someone was at the door and no one was there. I decided it was the wind. I looked out to the ocean. The wind howled. I saw the white caps, the wild waters. I was convinced I saw a woman standing on the edge of the shoreline holding a bundle in her arms. I'm convinced I tapped into some darker source, and Jane was attempting to warn me. The following day just as the sun was making its final descent, leaving behind a crimson glow, I walked along the shore, imbibed with enormous peace. I ended up at the creek. I happened to look down into the calm waters, and my peace ended. Down below was a young girl, her arms thrashing in an apparent struggle. I dove in off the rock to save the girl. Strangely enough, she was no longer there. I dove down under at least five or six times, and couldn't find her. Afterwards, I sat in the rocks catching my breath, waiting for her. Seagulls flew overhead, a few landed close to me. A blue heron perched close by. A deep sadness rushed over me as if I'd lost something profound I couldn't quite name.

These are just a few occurrences of unknown origin where I felt my mother's presence. Other times I'd wake to her voice in my head, saying my name. I was reminded then, of how she did this to me growing up as well. It was Jane who steered me in the right direction all along.

I wish I could provide you with more information about her. I wish I could describe a miracle or some healing that took place. I can vouch for the strangers, the procession to the beach, the baptizing. She had many followers then, and now. I can submit their experiences with Jane Wright, their testimonies. Whatever that means, I don't know.

As for me, she loved me and I always sensed it, even if I didn't spend much time with her. I forgave her and never held any ill will against her. When she was with me, I felt an overwhelming divine presence. And in her absence, the peace stayed with me, reverberated inside my soul. She spoke to me but without words, spoke to my soul, guiding me, admonishing me, and praising me. She fed my art and many of my most desirable paintings and sketches represent, somehow, my encounters, physical and spiritual, with

Jane Wright. My ears were closed, unfortunately, but she was there, and I'm convinced, now, it was Jane who saved me, and healed me of my addictions.

If you require further information or evidence, or if I should recall an event I've forgotten, I'll be sure to contact you.

Please, as much as possible, keep me updated regarding the investigative process and outcomes.

Sincerely Yours,

Helen Wright

Your Reverence, God does work in mysterious ways. I thought I was finished but left it unsealed as I needed to purchase a larger package to hold all the letters. I don't believe in coincidences. I was meant to leave it unsealed. I was seeking some sign and I do think it arrived.

Often times, when I had my room in the attic, I'd glance over at the place where the wallpaper used to be. Now it's painted over with no signs of its existence. After reading her journals, I suspect it wasn't so much the dingy wallpaper itself but her fear of being alone and abandoned by God, the fear of her own descent into a dark realm of sin and faithlessness. I think there was more to it, as I've felt it too, some darker presence at work.

As I've said, these past weeks I've been troubled trying to think of anything I might offer you, some evidence, some intercession or healing I'd witnessed. So, prior to a trip to the post office, I decided to take a walk along the shore. I happened to notice something unusual sticking out of the sand—not so uncommon as random items wind up in the Sound. But this one seemed especially odd for different reasons, which I'll disclose to you. I suspected something about it, an intuition, you might call it. I got up closer to it only to find a scrap of faded yellow wallpaper. My heart raced, as I considered the implications. When I stooped down to get a better look, I noticed the familiar pattern described so frequently in my mother's journal entries, the ivy swirling in and out of itself, that faded yellow, the vintage style paper. It fixed me to the spot, and I was bewitched. I thought to pick it up, but just as I was about to a wave rushed up and took it away. I watched it fight the incoming tide, try to plant itself back into the sand, and then retreat and succumb to a watery grave.

It seems unlikely that after all these years, that would be the same wallpaper. I tried to find some rationale for it, as many items are washed up and found on the shore.

And I might have dismissed it, except I know how fixated Jane had become, and how in her final stay in the attic, it tortured her so. I'm an art history major, and so I recognized the pattern, the trailing blossoms, crawling vertical branches and birds, a 17th century chinoiserie, an oriental design created to evoke simplicity and harmony, not what Jane described as "a labyrinth of creeping, evil tendrils. . .the trickery of lines, the vile optical deceit of soft expression."

I couldn't let it go, Your Reverence. I'm one who finds solace in the logical. And here I was completely and utterly enamored. It appeared, briefly, once more, and I followed it as it bobbed along on the waves, a meager scrap of paper no bigger than six inches in length, four in width, with its pointed edges jutting out, as if to pierce my soul. I should have felt threatened, uneasy. Instead, I was moved, stirred to solemnity, pacified as the salt water sprayed me, and the wind picked up, and it returned to me as I recalled a moment long ago in my mother's arms, when a light embraced me, and I swam in a dazzling brilliance.

I will end here with the strongest evidence I have of my mother, Jane Wright, and her divine presence, and the will of God, as it did with her, now working within me.

Yours Sincerely in Christ,
Helen Wright

The End

www.ingramcontent.com/pod-product-compliance
Lightning Source LLC
Chambersburg PA
CBHW060425260626
47161CB00005B/1794